# SUPER PAC
# DARK MONEY
# FRACKING

## PRAISE FOR STEWERT JAMES AND THE PARKER MOORE SERIES

*"James does a great job of setting the stage for politics and corruption ..."*

John Presley, Provost, Illinois State University

*"... based on true events."*

*Northern Express*

*"Sam comes alive in this book. She becomes a heroine to all."*

J. MacDonald, Harbor Springs

*"... eye-opening, especially in this election year."*

Sharon O., Kindle Addict

*"We want more Parker Moore!"*

J. Smith, Denver, Colorado

*"... fast-paced from the opening chapter."*

*Petoskey News Review*

*"These books will change the shape of elections for years to come."*

Friends @ The Carnegie

*"Should be on every airport counter in the country."*

*"Stewert James ... is a great read."*

OTHER BOOKS FROM MITCHELL STREET PRESS

**By STEWERT JAMES**

*Super PAC ~~Strikethrough~~*

*Super PAC Nine-Day Shadow*

*Super PAC Dark Money Fracking*

*The Shorts*

**By TOM RENKES AND JOHN PRESLEY**

*Two Lives Two Thousand Omens*

# SUPER PAC
# DARK MONEY
# FRACKING

Book 3 of the Parker Moore Series

# SUPER PAC DARK MONEY FRACKING

THE REDEMPTION OF PARKER MOORE

STEWERT JAMES

Enjoy!

MITCHELL STREET PRESS
PETOSKEY, MICHIGAN
WASHINGTON D.C.

Mitchell Street Press
Petoskey, Michigan
Washington D.C.

**www.stewertjames.com**



James, Stewert.
Super PAC dark money fracking : the redemption of Parker Moore / Stewert James. — Petoskey, Michigan : Mitchell Street Press [2014].

pages ; cm.
(Parker Moore series ; book 3)

ISBN: 978-0-9885011-4-0
1. Political action committees—United States—21st century—Fiction. 2. Hydraulic fracturing—Michigan—Fiction. 3. Hydraulic fracturing—United States—Fiction. 4. United States—Politics and government—Fiction. 5. Politicians—United States—Fiction. 6. Lobbying—United States—Fiction. 7. Foreign agents—United States—Fiction. 8. Citizens United—Fiction. 9. United States. National Security Agency—Fiction. 10. Political fiction. I. Title. II. Series: Parker Moore series ; bk. 3.

PS3610.A4547 S863 2014 2014947427
813/.6—dc23 1409

*Printed in the United States of America*
Second Printing

COVER & INTERIOR DESIGN BY TO THE POINT SOLUTIONS
www.tothepointsolutions.com

*To the people of the Great Lakes.*

*Cherish them forever.*

# ACKNOWLEDGMENTS

FIRST, I WOULD LIKE TO THANK THE PEOPLE OF FREDERIC and all those who make the Swamp a regular feature in their lives. The surrounding area is a snapshot of rural America looking for itself; however, many in Frederic like it just the way it is.

Second, thank you to my editor, Mary Jo, and the many family and friends—John, Sharon, Holly, Joey, Paul, and Christine—who help with pre-reading and critiquing the manuscripts. While not always easy, there would not be a completed novel without them.

To the communities of Petoskey and Harbor Springs, thank you for allowing me to show up at multiple doorsteps and venues with notebook in hand. As always, the people, places, and faces are real.

Thank you to the people who work the fracking grounds and the citizens who live among them, because right or wrong, life changes around you when big oil and gas come to town.

A big thank-you to the experts who shared their facts and opinions with me. They informed me that while they believe fracking has proven to be safe for many years, it absolutely pours poison into the earth and accidents do happen.

Finally, I want to pay homage to the Great Lakes. While other locales around the world constantly worry about drought and climate change, we have started to take these freshwater seas for granted; and as we continue to debate the global energy issue, perhaps it is time we simply slowed down and learned to live with what we have.

*The hours were long and the days empty. Except for prayers, the gain was nowhere to be seen for the local communities. Dust-parched lips in the spring and summer and cold, frigid hands and feet in the winter left a distasteful dread amongst all who worked on the wells and in the fields. There was no longer any local water. Trucks arrived with water—for the wells—and left with oil. Fewer and fewer trucks brought food and luxuries as promised.*

# ONE

**SUNDAY, APRIL 10**

"THEY PAVED PARADISE AND PUT UP A PARKING LOT, *ohhhh* …" a young woman was doing her best Joni Mitchell impression at open mic day at Roast & Toast. Parker and Sam Moore sat in the center booth, watching and singing along. The place was standing room only as the afternoon turned into evening. "You know," Parker leaned over to Sam's right ear, "she's not bad."

Sam just smiled and nodded without skipping a beat of the song she was trying to keep up with.

"What's new with you guys? Anybody die around you lately?" Mary asked as she pulled up a chair to the outside of their booth.

"God, no!" said Sam. "Do you believe it? It's like a curse."

The music had stopped as there was a change of singers. Music stands banged and guitars and people shuffled around at the front window area. Mary turned and grabbed the left arm of a man who was walking behind her as he headed toward the restrooms in the back of the coffeehouse. "Pat. You've got to meet these two. Sam and Parker Moore."

"How do you do?" Pat Coruthers stuck out his hand toward Parker. He was dressed in a dark blue suit and white dress shirt sans tie. Way out of place for local talent day in Petoskey during the off-season.

"Fine, thank you." Parker stood and clasped Coruthers' right hand. They looked each other square in the eyes and froze for a moment as their hands strained while they silently tested each other's strength.

"It's a pleasure." Coruthers released his grip and bent down to shake Sam's hand in a much more gentile fashion. "Have we met before?"

"Not that I remember. Mr. Coruthers was it?" Sam gave him the most cordial smile she could muster.

"Yes. Pat. Been a long day. I'm up here surveying."

"Land?" Sam asked.

"Well, yes. Land and real estate. It's time to put some money back into Michigan."

"Investor?" Sam pressed; still smiling.

"Energy. Resources we have in this state that will put people to work."

"You guys talk. I gotta get back to work." Mary retreated behind the counter to help at the cash register.

"Actually, we need to leave too. Mr. Coruthers, it's been a pleasure," Parker said as he stood up.

"The pleasure was all mine. I'll be back and forth from Grand Rapids. Perhaps we'll run into each other again."

"Perhaps. Enjoy the music," Parker said as he took Sam's hand and they walked toward the door.

*"In the early morning rain …"* the next seventeen-year-old Gordon Lightfoot wannabe was just beginning his performance.

Sam looked behind and around Parker to get a glimpse of Coruthers before she exited the restaurant. He had vanished.

"I wonder what kind of energy he's talking about." Sam's smile was gone; a determined look replaced it. She stared straight ahead as they walked briskly on Lake Street toward Howard Street.

"Who knows? Don't go getting a bee in your bonnet. He's got money and everybody up here wants it." Parker was trying to keep up with Sam. He always walked on the street side, in his normal chivalrous manner, but Sam generally outpaced him which forced him to always be catching up.

Sam stopped. Parker ran into her and had to grab her so she wouldn't fall.

"Kiss my ass." Sam resumed walking. "A bee in my bonnet? Where the hell'd you pull that one from? Some Cary Grant movie on Turner today?" Sam was half serious and half laughing.

Parker grabbed her hand and pulled her toward him. At first, Sam was stunned.

"Yes, dahling," Parker said in his best Cary Grant imitation. "Judy, Judy, Judy! Can we now move to Paris and forget all the little people?" Parker was down on one knee and held his folded hands to his chest.

"Oh, shut up!" Sam pushed Parker over, onto his back, and laughed.

"Hey!" Parker scrambled to his feet. "I have to run over to Kathi's and hang a shelf before her grand opening tomorrow."

"Fine," Sam turned, grabbed Parker's face with both hands, and kissed him. "Come on up to my room when you get home. I'll have nothin' on but the radio," she said in her best Mae West impersonation.

As the two parted ways in the middle of Lake Street at Pennsylvania Park, a black Escalade with darkened windows drove between them. Pat Coruthers only looked at Sam Moore.

# TWO

"A LITTLE MORE UP ON THE LEFT. NO. NO. NOW BACK DOWN on the right. There! Okay, now center it." Kathi Morris was directing Parker as he tried to hang the shelf behind the counter of the new store.

"Kathi, this thing's heavy," Parker said as he struggled to keep the shelf up.

"That's why you lift weights. Now, hold it! Let me mark it," Kathi's lyrical voice was stern as she readied her store for its grand opening, fulfilling a twenty-year dream.

As soon as she was done, Parker set the shelf down and started drilling. "So, Kathi, I assume you found your investors?" he asked as the drill slowly made its way through plasterboard, wood lath, and into the cinder block. One-hundred-year-old walls were always a mystery when drilling.

"Sure did. Nice guy from Grand Rapids. He recently bought the building and was looking to finance a new tenant. Something about 'creating jobs' and, and, um 'an entrepreneurial stewardship' he called it."

"Grand Rapids?" Parker kept working on setting the anchors into the wall.

"Yes. Man named Coruthers. Pat Coruthers."

"Really? I just met him over at Roast & Toast. Says he's into 'energy resources.'"

"I don't know about that. I just know I have a store." Kathi held out her arms, smiling.

"*We* have a store, thank you very much," Kathi's partner, Pam, chimed in.

Parker placed the shelf on the screws he'd anchored into the wall. Yesterday, he had installed the light fixtures and sound system; now it was time to soak it all in. He turned to survey the room. It was a classic antique and consignment shop for people with Victorian homes or cottages, which describes half of the Petoskey area. Big, plush sofas; antique sideboards; china cabinets; and a plethora of chairs, pillows, and lamps filled most of the space. There were displays of lavender soaps and assorted hand towels. Local artwork and old window shutters filled up the wall space. It looked as if *Coastal Living* magazine was going to arrive for a cover shoot.

"Yep, Kathi. This is a gem." Parker put his tools down and looked outside toward Lake Street. "Pat Coruthers," he whispered to himself.

"Stop running! Nobody will hurt you!" A man in tan dress slacks yelled as he chased after an old-timer in light blue Carhartt coveralls. "Shit!" he exclaimed as his Johnston & Murphy shoes splashed through Goose Creek.

The old man from Frederic kept turning his head to glance at the man chasing him. He had no intention of slowing down. His best chance was to get to either County Road 612 or M-72. Either way it was a few miles.

"Look, old man! This is stupid. I just want to ask you some questions."

The forest was becoming darker as the white pines gave way to cedars and tamaracks. Low-hanging branches from the scrub pine nicked at the old-timer's sleeves. He kept a steady pace. Since he'd hunted and fished along the Manistee River for better than sixty years, there wasn't much territory in these twenty square miles he didn't know. The gas line was now hundreds of yards behind him to the north and west. His best bet was a hike to 72. The road was busier, and he had a better chance to get a ride. Ron and Sandy's store was closed, so he'd try the Eagles Club.

Silence from behind. The old-timer stopped and listened. In early April, even after a light winter, there were still piles of snow on the river trails away from the sun. He slowed to a walk, being careful not to make tracks. He walked around snow and mud and on brown and yellow grasses and sea-green lichens. *No city fella's goin' to track me*, he thought to himself. Recent logging had removed most of the timber near Goose Creek Road, leaving only a small buffer zone along the river for tourists. The path was becoming choked with snow, making it easy to track.

Nightfall was only a few hours away, and he wasn't dressed for the cold in his light coveralls. His breath was hard and turning to frost in the late afternoon. *Never expected to be doin' this. Just tryin' to find my bait pile.* His rusted out Ford F-150 was parked on 612, a good three miles north of where he was now. He'd have to chance it.

He peered westward, through the woods, looking over the clear-cutting. *No way he's followed me.* He began to walk out of the woods, trying to keep a low profile and stopping to listen every ten yards or so. *Two hundred yards to Goose Creek Road.* Another ten yards; a look and listen. The sun was low over the hills to the southwest and disappearing quickly. *Be back home by eight.*

The report of the gun was quieted by the suppressor. The old-timer never heard or saw the barrel's flash due to the glare of the sun. He went down like he was hit with a hammer.

"Old son of a bitch. Jesus!" he said as he looked down at the corpse. His tan slacks were covered in mud and his shoes were soaked. They'd never be the same.

*He would watch the helicopters come and go, delivering men and women in lab coats. The arrival of more lab coats often meant delays in field work. Something needed to be adjusted or tested. In the last several years, fluids discharged from the wells killed the crops. Some teens dropped cigarettes when startled by elders, and a field caught fire. Allah has spoken, some said. We are doing the work of the infidels, others noted. What else could we do to survive? We invited this torture and now we must figure a way to either live with it or rid ourselves of it.*

# THREE

**MONDAY, APRIL 11**

HE STARED OUT THE WINDOW OF THE BAR HARBOR BAR in Harbor Springs. The four inches of snow from an overnight squall had been plowed into piles around the parking lots. No boats at the docks and no tourists roaming the water's edge; the flurries continued. A gray sky covered Little Traverse Bay and the small, quaint natural harbor made for a one-dimensional monochrome picture. Just like his mood.

John Stanley, billionaire and owner of Stanley Limited, sipped his Bombay martini as he waited for his lobbyist to finish in the bathroom. "Hannah, can you bring us another? Thanks," Stanley said, holding up his almost empty glass.

"Dry as the first?" Hannah asked.

"How about holding the vermouth upright over the glass and hoping some falls in?"

"Two olives?"

"None. They take up too much space."

"Got it," Hannah yelled as she grabbed for the Bombay gin between the Tanqueray and Beefeaters.

The man Stanley was waiting for walked out of the restroom. He was dressed in jeans and a tweed sport coat—never a black suit or tie-of-the-month from the latest designer.

"What the hell? I pay you enough, why do you dress like that?" Stanley said, perturbed. "And, what the hell were you doing in there so long, painting the stalls?"

"Old man prostate, John. Oh, that's right. You don't have one."

Stanley's lobbyist squeezed into the high booth perched against the long wall of windows to afford the best view of the harbor.

"Here ya go," Hannah said as she placed a new cocktail napkin under the martini. "You ready?"

"Yes. Oban. Neat," the man in the tweed coat said with a smile.

Hannah walked away, whistling "Iris" by the Goo Goo Dolls; the song that was playing over the speakers in the bar.

Stanley leaned over the table and whispered, "I pay a fortune and you treat me like shit."

"John, you're a billionaire. No one treats you like shit. We all make you a ton of money so … so we take liberties."

"Here ya go, Parker. How's Sam?"

"She's good, Hannah. Just moved into new offices."

"Tell her hello."

Hannah walked away. Parker turned back toward John Stanley.

"Are you going to do this for me, Moore?" Stanley asked.

"Maybe."

"I need this, Moore. I'm eighty years old and dying a slow death of idleness and martinis. This is the last business deal I wish to make." John Stanley had tears in his eyes as he held the martini glass in between the thumb and middle finger of his right hand. As he brought it up to his mouth, the small tremors of Parkinson's were evident.

"I promised Sam I'd never get into this game again. Hell, I promised myself. I only did it for you, John. You know I haven't cashed any of your checks. They all went directly to the kids."

"That's your decision, Moore. This will be my legacy," Stanley said as he set his drink down and looked to his left, out the window at the gray sky. The flurries had slowed.

"Okay, John. I'll be your bag man." Parker Moore sipped his scotch and shared John Stanley's gaze out the window.

Pat Coruthers walked the square of land that he had received approval for. As he walked over tufts of dry grass and light, chalk-green lichens, he read the papers in his hands. Leather boots kept his feet dry as he headed into the swamps of Goose Creek. As he approached the thick growth of black spruce, some white pine and scrub, he stopped and turned his iPad to look at the surveyed map. He found north and placed a paper map in his hands directionally appropriate to his position. He noticed to the east a thirty-acre parcel owned by a consortium of attorneys from Ohio and Indiana. South and west of that was state land. To the north of the attorneys' land was an empty canoe and fishing campground, then seven parcels of land equaling twenty-five acres, and finally, state land again. His placement in the swampy area was perfect for another test site. The pipeline easement allowed the state an easy decision for lease—especially for what his investors in the super PAC were willing to pay.

He began to walk again. The papers were tucked safely in his jacket pocket as he used his iPad to check any recent e-mails. Coruthers was well past Goose Creek, which was five feet at its widest part and only up to his knees at its deepest depth. As he jumped through the creek, he had noticed a couple of brook trout streak out of the small eddies. Goose Creek emptied into the Manistee River several hundred yards south and east of his position. As he turned to look back at the creek, just before he walked into the dense forest, he thought about the fly-fishing he did as a kid with his father. He had tried and tried to perfect the art of the 10-and-2 cast but never did. His father would ignore him as he tangled the line over cedar sweeps and under dead-heads; resentment building slowly over time.

It wasn't just the fly-fishing. It was life. His father was a ruthless businessman—all about money and profit. "Making money every day was better than spending it," was his dad's motto. Now, Pat Coruthers was no different. Fracking was going to succeed, and he already owned half the state leases—or so he would like to think. The super PAC Resources For All (RFA) funded him. As CEO and President of Grand Rapids Resources (GRR), his ownership was becoming a self-induced entitlement.

The land in Frederic Township, right on the Crawford and Kalkaska County lines between County Road 612 and state highway M-72, was a stroke of genius. The counties needed the revenue, and Frederic was home to one of the most active Michigan militias wanting no one around. He could test here with virtually no worries. After all, the site upriver was running and no one knew anything about it–money took care of that.

He walked. The air was quiet and about thirty-eight degrees. The sun's angles were changing as the days lengthened. As he entered the bogs, he saw some snow was still packed underneath the dense spruce and scrub pine. A few towering white pines were the only remnants of the nineteenth-century logging days. Some red pine that needed more light had grown after the majestic white pines were clear cut. Coruthers looked up and left as he entered the woods and spied a black bear. He was downwind of the bear and walking so slowly, he caused no attention to himself, plus the bear was busy ripping into downed trees for termites and other edibles. Coruthers backtracked softly. He snapped a twig after about twenty feet and the bear turned; glaring, it huffed once before returning to its browse for food. Coruthers turned and walked quietly away toward another entry into the forest.

He was now standing in a native grass meadow surrounded by black spruce. Crows flew overhead as chickadees and Pine Siskins danced from tree to tree. The area was only a shell of the hundred-foot tall white pines that stretched from Lake Huron to Lake Michigan. It was said that you could walk for days and never see the sun. The only trails were game trails and some old hunting and fishing trails.

As he walked closer to the confluence of Goose Creek and the Manistee, he could see the ancient stumps. Hundreds covered the acres around him. The Manistee, to his east, was much deeper before the logging. Erosion and weathering of the banks made the once deep and mighty river a shallow fisherman's paradise—more like an English chalk stream. Proud fishermen with stringers of grayling trout in gray-sienna daguerreotypes were a distant memory. Today, only the brook trout and imported German browns survived the silted streams; however, the area had finally reached some re-generation. Bobcat, bears, turkeys, and even some wolves joined the white-tailed deer and the rest of the surviving flora and fauna.

He reached the confluence and ran his right boot over the pebbles in the shallow eddy. His business would be invisible as he continued his goal toward an energy monopoly funded by the super PAC for their political gain. With the federal elections over, their money went to local influence, and the political capital spent earned several times that on real enterprise. The only thing Pat Coruthers knew was that the super PAC funding his company had accounts in fifty states, camouflaged money from around the world. And HSBC was the perfect bank since they didn't care. Oil and gas funded the super PAC, which in turn influenced the politics to make billions from oil and gas, then more could be given to the super PAC, and the cycle continued. Coruthers didn't care about the politics because he was becoming one of the super-rich faster than he ever thought possible.

He smiled and looked at the two streams. He'd enjoy coming here and supervising the well. It would be good to fish again. He turned to walk back to his car that was parked on the shoulder of Goose Creek Road; he kept his head down as he walked so as not to step deep into a bog. All the rhetoric over fracking was useless. He knew the business and it felt safe enough to him, after all, it was more about the energy needs of the locals than anything else—besides, it wasn't his backyard. The common folk wouldn't understand the chemical process and didn't need to. It was safe as long as people had jobs and could begin spending money.

As he stepped into the clearing for the current natural gas pipeline that ran north and south between the woods and Goose Creek Road, he noticed his footprints bubbled underneath him with each slow step. The water table was essentially at the surface, but no worries. With the faltering economy and a conservative Republican administration, the time was now. There were fewer hunters and even fewer law enforcement.

*Where the hell is that grave?* he thought. The old-timer was going to make trouble; it was not the first time someone had to be silenced in the name of progress. He probably wouldn't be missed and the old-timer's trailer in Frederic just might be useful.

Coruthers turned one more time just before he walked through the last edge of trees onto the road. He bit his lower lip as he gazed at the area he had just covered. *This'll work. Yup. This'll work.* He crossed through the new-growth red pines and up onto Goose Creek Road at the culvert. He looked up and down the gravel road that ran north and south. Three hours and not another person or vehicle seen. Gas prices at four dollars a gallon didn't allow for a lot of leisure travel to the north anymore—just quiet roads.

He kicked the dirt from his boots before he stepped inside the black Escalade; he buckled his seatbelt, turned the ignition, and rolled down the window. The local Fox News radio affiliate came over the speakers, spooking a doe and a very early fawn from the other side of the road. The doe was probably still caching the fawn in the brush, and the mother's hollow fur was still winter gray. The two deer turned, sprinted in front of the parked SUV, and with a steady gait and one quick leap, they disappeared into the brush.

Patrick Coruthers put the black urban truck into drive and headed north on Goose Creek Road toward County Road 612. It would be a short jaunt over to Frederic and his meeting at the Swamp. He'd be home by the wee hours of Tuesday morning. Whistling as he listened to the news and the SUV kicked up gravel, he hit 50 mph and figured that was a good speed to have some fake four-wheel fun. He passed a couple of turkeys alongside the road as he neared the blacktop—but never slowed down.

# FOUR

"SIR, MIGHT I REMIND YOU IT'S APRIL, AND WE'VE ALREADY had two weeks of seventy-degree weather. There have been more than five hundred and thirty tornadoes recorded in the U.S. this year, and we're only two weeks into spring!" Sam was sitting at the table giving her testimony in the Frederic Township Hall.

Hans "Dutch" Van Der Knacht, a Republican State Senator from Hudsonville, held court, leaning forward on the four-foot long folding table covered with a white, plastic tablecloth while his two staff members whispered in his left ear as they leaned forward in their own chairs behind him.

"Mrs. Moore, perhaps the seasons are just changing. Perhaps it's an anomaly that occurred many times before recorded history. What do you say to that?" Dutch sat back and waited for an answer.

"I have no way to defend that remark, Senator. I am here as a representative of our group against fracking, and I can speak to the data we currently have. I suggest that scientists the world over and the latest public opinion polls show a definite belief the climate is changing at an accelerated rate due to manmade circumstances. Fossil fuels are the chief concern, Senator. We understand your ..."

"Be careful, Mrs. Moore," the Senator leaned forward again. "What you think is my opinion is not. I am here to make jobs and provide an economic opportunity for those in this room."

Applause rang out from the seats in the back—mostly men who would rather work than spend their idle time collecting unemployment. Pat Coruthers and his associate, both dressed in blue jeans and all-weather North Face coats, sat in their midst.

"Senator, if I may, we understand your wish is to allow the proliferation of oil and natural gas exploration with an unchecked mandate. We also understand a company within your constituency, which is also a political supporter, GRR, owns most of the state leases for this exploration. We consider your opinions and the reason for holding this hearing ludicrous since you have a substantial bias."

"Watch yourself, missy." Dutch was standing and leaning on the table with his right hand and pointing his left index finger at Sam Moore. "This hearing is exactly what it is intended to be: a fair informational sharing of facts, testimony, and citizen response to a very necessary energy policy."

"Excuse me, Senator. I apologize if my remarks are more than candid. It is my right to express opinion just as it is for everyone else in this room."

"Indeed." He sat down. "But, everyone else in this room is in favor of what you're speaking against." He smiled and looked at the standing-room only audience. "These people would like to work. They want to prosper, just as you do. Now, is that so bad?"

"At what price, Senator? The ruination of the environment around them? Short-term gain has been here before, sir. Lumber. Long-term sustainability of this area's natural resources would go a long way to continue a resurrection of tourism, hunting, and fishing. In fact, the fishing hasn't actually recovered from the lumber-baron days at the turn of the century. The allowance of fracking would create an unknown chemical wash that could destroy this environment forever."

"Is there anyone else who would like to speak?"

"Senator, excuse me. I have the floor and my time is not up."

"I believe we've heard all you've said, Mrs. Moore, and all you would continue to say."

The crowd cheered loudly. Coruthers and his associate remained quiet. They scanned the room to account for everyone they knew or didn't know.

"Go back to Petoskey!" someone shouted from the back of the room.

"You don't belong here, honey," an elderly woman sitting behind Sam said softly.

Sam kept a steady demeanor and said, "Senator, my husband's family has been in the area since the 1930s. In fact, his father is buried in the local cemetery."

Silence in the room.

The senator cleared his throat. "Well, we've still heard enough. Thank you, Mrs. Moore." Dutch Van Der Knacht grabbed his gavel and hit the table three times. "We're adjourned. Now, I suspect I'll see most of you over at the Swamp."

The crowd stood and cheered. When the applause ended, "bitch," "rich bitch," and "beer time" could be heard over the murmur of multiple conversations.

The senator stood and shook the hands of several people who came up to him before he could even walk around the table. Most were dressed in jeans, overalls, and flannel shirts–even the women. Frederic was a proud community that didn't take to people from outside its boundaries telling them how to think. Even if they didn't like the government, the senator played perfectly into their favor.

Sam Moore was disgruntled. She sighed and packed her briefcase with the papers before her. By the time she was done and looked around, the room was empty; and to make it worse, the older woman sitting behind her turned the lights out as she left. Sam sat in the dark.

In a remote area of Turkmenistan, Sir Edward sat in his private jet on the tarmac. He looked out the window at the wellheads, drill platforms, towers, and trucks that dotted the landscape. People moved among the machinery as if they were ants in a field of black grass. As far as his eyes could take him, there was no life as he knew it. No homes. No shops. No villages, cities, or towns. No hedgerows or rose gardens. Just a black-metal landscape. Even the sun worked its way through a gray sky.

He smiled as the data on his phone attested to increasing oil and gas prices. He moved his thumb over the screen and reviewed the upcoming votes on anti-fracking legislation in various locales throughout the United States. His thumb moved over the screen again and a face and number appeared. He swiped to answer.

"Yes?" was the answer.

"How did it go?"

"Well."

"Was she there?" Sir Edward gazed out the window as he accepted a Hendrick's martini from the attendant.

"Yes."

"Any threats?"

"Not that we can discern."

"This would be one of our biggest markets. It mustn't go awry."

"No reason to think it will."

"Right. Keep it that way," said Sir Edward. His phone vibrated in his hand. He pushed the screen again. "John, how are you? Thanks for returning my call. Do you have a minute?"

† † †

Parker was in his studio working on research for John Stanley. Attempting the impossible was always possible for Parker, but it was his soul he most worried about. While making a complete life change over the last several years (Sam called it living an *authentic* life), Parker wasn't afraid of the project or the work needed to accomplish John Stanley's dream, he was afraid of what he would have to return to: plane rides, political action committees, quiet backroom meetings, dishonest politics, power, and money. Many would relish this work and the lifestyle, but in the long run, a deep toll is taken on the spirit—at least on Parker Moore's spirit.

Cutty Sark was the current scotch on his writing desk. A break from single malts usually meant that writing was slow. And it was. Parker had been comfortable working on his daughter's house, visiting his newly engaged son and fiancée at George Washington Law in Washington D.C., and fostering his youngest through his first term at the University of Michigan. Blimpy Burgers had never tasted so good.

The call from John Stanley had sparked a great deal of soul searching and long evening discussions with Sam. Once a conclusion was reached, that Stanley's ideas were of great cause and help to the surrounding community, Sam agreed to relinquish her worries to the confidence of Parker's judgment. His life recovery intact, it was a way to help others with a skillset few if any in Northern Michigan had.

Parker hadn't slept much Sunday night, but he felt confident after their conversation. Right or wrong, he felt alive.

"Hello? You in your studio?" Sam yelled down the stairs.

"Hey, doll. I'll be right up."

Kali and Keeper ran down the basement steps as soon as Sam opened the door.

"Yo! Hey, get the hell outta here, you guys. You know better than that." Parker herded the two cats upstairs as he turned off the lights and secured the basement door.

"Sam?"

"Up here. I'm changing. I feel dirty."

"Dirty? What happened?" Parker made his way up the stairs to their bedroom.

"I got politically trounced by a master of politics."

"Ole Dutch?"

"You got it. What a son of a bitch." Sam worked at her dress pants and camisole. "I know I said all the right things, but those people don't want any part of me or the cause."

"Power and money." Parker whispered loudly as he sat in the chaise looking out toward Little Traverse Bay and Lake Michigan.

"You're goddamn right. Mostly money. Do you know how much this company—what's their name? GRR?—is going to make if fracking works? Do you know what's going to happen to the rivers, streams, and lakes around those bastards in Frederic?"

"They only see the green."

"All of the Zen we practice isn't helping me with this one," sighed Sam.

"Maybe it will all work out. Maybe there will be an alternative."

"Well, it better be quick because the remainder of those leases opens up soon."

"I know. And the pro-fracking websites are predicting greater profits and oil-and-gas riches beyond the Saudis' and Russians'."

Sam sat on the bed. She had changed into her bamboo yoga pants and was pulling a loose t-shirt over her head.

"Am I wrong, Parker? Are we wrong? Should we be on the other side of this one? Those people in Frederic haven't had jobs in decades."

"I don't know, Sam. On the one hand, the people up here need work. They need the money. But, they moved up here for other reasons–especially in Frederic. They don't like government or authority. Once the money gets old or dries up, you wonder if they'll hate the hand that's feeding them." Parker had his hands folded behind his head as he stared out the window.

Sam stood and moved over to the floor-to-ceiling window and leaned against the left edge as she gazed out at the bay and the lake. "It's so frustrating." Sam turned and looked at Parker. "Honey, I may need more of your help on this one. You wouldn't have been trapped in that meeting like I was today."

Parker was deep in thought. "An alternative," he said softly. "Yes! An alternative!" He stood up and hugged Sam.

"Okay. I'll take that, but I have no idea what you're talking about."

"John Stanley's legacy. Why not in Frederic? It's perfect."

"It is? Parker, there's one two-lane road and nothing else besides the Swamp. There are places in Alaska and the Amazon more commercialized."

"I know. That's what makes this perfect. Can you imagine the press? The construction? The jobs? The fact that it would only add tourists to the lakes, rivers, and streams—and not poison." Parker sat back down.

"Slow down," said Sam. "You don't even know who you're up against."

"Sam? Honey? Are you kidding? After the last several years and what we've lived through? Well, what I've lived through ..."

"So, what? We work both ends? Anti-fracking and pro-industry? Seems like an oxymoron."

"Perhaps," Parker said as he gazed at the bay. "Perhaps."

A black Escalade was parked on Williams just north of Mitchell Street. The driver's window was cracked enough for a telephoto camera lens to peak out. The scene of Sam and Parker behind the full-length window was easy to capture.

"They're home. No signs of anything except them talking," the man said into his Bluetooth.

"Be patient. We don't need another fatality, unless it's absolutely necessary. I'll be back up north in a few days."

"Take your time. Nothing's going to happen till then."

"I may have to fly to Dubai to make sure everyone's on the same page. So, again, don't hurt anyone. You follow?"

"Yes."

"Later."

The phone call ended.

It was a foggy morning in Dubai. Members of Resources For All, the super PAC, were sitting down to an early breakfast in their private suite. Although the name of the super PAC had been changed, except for one new face, everyone and everything remained the same.

"Let's begin, shall we?" Sir Edward Framingham had finished his eggs and bangers. The coffee was hot and steam rose from the white mug with **RFA** emblazoned in red on it; the mug sat on the marble end table to his side. "Since the elections went against us in the U.S. Presidential race, we continue to pursue our profit potential elsewhere. Several states have moved further into the arena of hydraulic fracturing, and we have established ourselves in all of them. You'll notice that in each state, we've given support to the appropriate political parties who are, excuse the pun, carrying our water." Sir Edward smiled as he looked around the room. The other eight members continued to eat as they listened.

"Please, Sir Edward," began the woman from Norway, "we're still feeling the sting of losing our colleague from Texas. Are we better protected in this venture?"

"Yes. We've all voted to not incorporate any Americans in our group–for now. Our Russian partner, Mr. Evgeny, is in charge of security, and I have lived through the NSA's attempt to ruin my company and my reputation. "

"But, the way we utilize our resources in the U.S.—is everything protected?" The woman from Norway pressed on.

The others in the room stopped chewing to await Sir Edward's answer.

"Yes, as I said before. Our Cayman accounts have all been closed, and new ones have been opened in Hong Kong through numerous 501(c)(4) ventures. Each political ally in the U.S. is protected. As are we. So far, we are in Pennsylvania, Oklahoma, Wyoming, California, and North Dakota. We will be exiting Wyoming and transferring to Indiana. The Wyoming legislature has become an unfriendly place, even after several hundred thousand dollars. Right now, North Dakota and Michigan seem to be the most favorable."

"We have security on the ground in each location," added Evgeny.

The partner from Canada was uneasy in his chair. "Please, excuse my hesitancy, but we were guaranteed security last time and it almost cost all of us. Our friend Mr. Reegan is in a U.S. federal prison, and you, Sir Edward, had to withstand horrible public humiliation and legal pressures. How do we know the NSA isn't still watching and listening?"

"Well, for one, we have no detainees this time around, so there is no one to rescue, and Evgeny's genius was to embed our messages and codes within the— what do they call it, Evgeny?—chatter of the continued uprisings in the Middle East." Sir Edward was confident as he responded. His legs were crossed comfortably and his hands rested on the sofa at his sides. "Most importantly, we kept everything as it was. Except for our security issues and Mr. Reegan taking a fall in his country, along with several politicos and one justice, the laws remain unchanged. If we were to move, more suspicion would be brought to bear."

"Very well. And the staff of our facility?" asked the Norwegian.

"Cleared," noted Evgeny. "We brought them all from Russia. Ex-KGB and GRU. Well paid now. No problem."

"Our future profits for the super PAC should be in the realm of a billion dollars a month if all goes well around the world. Please, you must all have forgotten. We're concentrating our resources in the states and local governments, not the Federal government of the United States; the local people are always naïve. Any other questions?" Sir Edward looked around the room. All were done eating and were sitting back, sipping coffee or tea. "Very well. I will have our Michigan liaison visit us this week to further assure the competence of our latest endeavor. Good morning to you all."

The group members began small discussions amongst themselves. Sir Edward moved toward the windows and surveyed the city below, still mired in fog. He motioned for Evgeny to join him.

"Yes?"

"We are making sure all is kept quiet?"

"Yes. No mistakes."

"And in Turkmenistan, Uzbekistan, and Azerbaijan?"

"Everywhere."

"Fine then. Thank you for taking over."

*The poppy fields were gone. He could look out over the horizon and see nothing but towers and wellheads. Instead of a village, he saw trailers and pole buildings. The old way of life was extinct. Nomads turned sedentary and villagers were slaves. Anger was swelling. Uprisings around the world were the only vicarious methods of surviving. Perhaps someday here; perhaps an uprising where the infidels were.*

# FIVE

TUESDAY, APRIL 12

"JOHN, YOU WANNA COME UP HERE?" JOHN MANSFIELD was in his typical attire: tattered sweater and tie loosened at the neck. He was using the speaker phone to call John Brooks three floors below him. Newspapers and clippings from around the world were scattered over his desk and floor.

"Sure, chief. Be right there."

John Brooks took a gulp of warm coffee and clicked off his email. When at rest, the computer-screen image was a photo of Parker Moore and him fishing the Manistee River. As he pushed away from his desk, Brooks looked out the window at the morning sun bursting through the trees that surrounded the building in Fort Meade, Maryland. He set his cup down, but then grabbed it for a warm-up. The staff kitchen was right by the elevator.

He couldn't help but think about his friend Parker Moore, who lived for sunrises like this when fishing. Brooks smiled as he walked out of his office. He poured some coffee from the Bunn coffeemaker in the kitchen and walked the twenty feet to the elevator. Just as he pushed the button, the door opened.

"Chief?"

"Come on in. We're going down."

Brooks's attire was the opposite of his boss's. His pressed black slacks, starched white shirt, and navy blue tie made John Mansfield look like a janitor.

"What's up?" Brooks sipped the hot coffee.

"You may be able to tell us."

"Us?"

"The group's back together."

"THE group or the GROUP?" Brooks asked, smiling at his boss who stood motionless.

John Mansfield didn't respond to the humor. "The Super PAC."

"So, THE BIG group."

"We've decoded some chatter from Bahrain, where our navy is docked. First take is some natural gas and oil developments tied to our old friends in Dubai."

"I thought that group went away after the conviction and public crucifixion of half our government."

The elevator door opened deep below the NSA building. The two men exited and passed through a security area staffed with heavily armed men in dark blue suits. As they progressed around the circular hallway, they came to the unlabeled briefing room.

"They didn't," Mansfield said as he stopped before opening the door. "And until a couple of months ago, we got lazy."

"But why me?"

"You'll see," Mansfield answered as he opened the door.

† † †

Pat Coruthers hung up the phone and climbed out of bed. He hit the shower and began packing for a trip he wasn't expecting so quickly.

"What the hell are you doing and where are you going?" his wife asked as she rolled over in bed. "What time is it?"

"It's seven thirty. I have to catch a plane."

She rolled back over. "Fine. Call me when you get wherever you get." She was used to his trips.

Coruthers was methodically, but quickly, packing his carry-on while the best suit was out of the closet, hanging on the valet at the ready. His mind was already halfway around the world.

† † †

Tim Johnson, Director of Public Safety, pulled into his parking spot behind the Petoskey City Hall. The morning was clear and sunny, but the temperature hovered in the low thirties. Frost from each breath emanated from Johnson as he huffed his way up the back stairs.

"Morning, Cindy," he said as he blew past his secretary's office.

"Morning," she yelled back. "You've got a …"

"Shit, Moore. What the hell are you doing here so early? Somebody die?"

"… visitor." Cindy finished as she looked at the papers on her desk.

"Tim. Tim. Now is that how you greet everyone on a fine day like this?" Parker Moore was sitting in Tim Johnson's chair.

"Only you, Parker. Only you," Johnson said. "Now, get outta my chair and get me some coffee."

"You got it."

Parker went down the hall and started a fresh pot. Tim Johnson hung his tan trench coat behind his door and settled in his chair. The harbor behind him was empty. The resorters and summer tourists were still in Florida and other warm locales south of the Mason-Dixon Line.

"Here ya go, boss. Fresh and strong." Parker set two mugs down on Johnson's desk.

"So, what's up?" Johnson asked as he took a mug and blew softly to cool the hot, black liquid as the steam warmed his face.

"Do you know that new store that just opened over on Lake, next to White Caps?"

"Yeah. Cottage something. The wife was already in, buying stuff."

"Well, this might be a coincidence, but the owner of the building was up from Grand Rapids the other day and he drives a black Escalade."

"So do a lot of people around here and Harbor Springs," Johnson replied snidely as he turned his computer on.

"Yeah, but this one's been parked outside our house, over on Williams Street, watching." Parker sat back in the leather chair in the corner of Johnson's office.

"The conspiracy void of the last year getting to you, Parker? I suppose the next thing you're going to tell me is they have guns and may want to assassinate you."

"No—well, not yet. Look, I saw the guy drive by Sam and me the other day. He owns the building Kathi's store is in, and other real estate in town. And, he's also into gas and oil something or other. It's just a hunch, but with Sam trying to be the truthsayer of fracking, I think this guy's up to no good. And that car, or one like it, was outside our house last night. I saw it when Sam and I were—"

"That's good enough."

"Talking. We were *talking*. I didn't say anything to Sam, but it was there."

"Plate?"

"No."

"Person?"

"No."

"Identifying marks or custom features we would notice?"

"No."

"Okay then. Thanks for the coffee. We'll wait."

"Good enough. See ya, Tim."

"Cindy!" Johnson yelled as Parker walked out of his office. "Make sure Parker gets some extra patrols the next few nights. Add Williams Street to somebody's assignment."

"You got it, Parker," Cindy said as Parker walked by.

"Thanks, Cindy." Parker turned and yelled down the hall, "Thanks, chief!"

"Where the hell's the newspaper?" Johnson yelled back.

"What is that?" five-year-old Michael asked his seven-year-old sister Sarah, as they walked to the school bus stop on Cameron Bridge Road just north and west of Frederic.

"Ewww. I don't know," she said as she stared over the bridge into the Manistee River.

"It looks like the stuff from Grandpa's boat motor at the lake."

Michael and Sarah watched the pink, blue, and green sheen flow from around the bend about fifty feet in front of them and down under the bridge they were standing on. It was continuous with no break or end in sight.

"Good morning, Mr. Brooks. Mr. Mansfield."

"Ma'am."

"Please sit." She pointed to two chairs on the back side of the round table. The other five members were looking at their tablets and the monitors around the room.

The Chairperson waited for Brooks and Mansfield to settle into their seats. "Thank you for coming down on such short notice. Mr. Brooks, we believe you'll be the lead on this one, assuming Mr. Mansfield approves?" She looked at Mansfield.

He nodded yes.

"Okay," started Brooks. "This what?"

"Here." She pointed to a sixty-inch monitor behind her. On the monitor appeared a map. "Michigan."

"Okay," John Brooks sat forward in his chair and folded his hands on the table. His chair was rocked forward on the two front legs.

"After the Presidential election in 2012, and everything settled down from the Supreme Court through Congress, we took a deep breath as we went after Sir Edward Framingham, his holdings, and assets. We were successful to a point, but the public has a short memory and eventually he outlasted the negative publicity and pressure. Then, as the civil unrest continued in Bahrain and Syria, we began to hear lots of noise, so we sent the CIA and NSA in to sort it out. Embedded in the chatter, one of our analysts found a threaded code to money and influence being peddled through a company in Grand Rapids, Michigan, here, called Grand Rapids Resources or GRR." She pointed to details on the map. "GRR specializes in obtaining leases for oil and natural gas drilling through hydraulic fracturing."

"In this case, we believe it's all natural gas," added John Mansfield.

"Yes, John, we hypothesize that Michigan is the next great leap for our boys and girls from Dubai. The state's economy and government are ripe for the picking." The former Secretary of State walked around the table toward John Brooks.

"How can these guys be active already, after their second-in-command was imprisoned, and the public outcry resonated all the way through the Supreme Court?" John Brooks was puzzled.

She bent down and looked into Brooks's eyes. "They've retooled with some new people, and the Supreme Court's Citizens United decision has yet to be overturned by new legislation. In other words, we still can't touch their money. And that total is about one trillion dollars in combined assets. We don't see any of it going toward Washington at this point, but it's going somewhere."

John Mansfield stood up and walked over to the monitor. "The threaded reference keeps referring to Frederic, Michigan." He looked at the map.

John Brooks laughed out loud.

"Something funny, Mr. Brooks?" The Chairperson smiled back.

"Have you ever been to Frederic?" Brooks could barely contain himself. His chair was now rocked backward.

"You have?"

"Yes. Parker Moore took me fishing there, along the Manistee River."

"Parker Moore?" She looked at Mansfield. "Again, with Moore?"

Mansfield shrugged his shoulders as he looked at her.

"Mr. Brooks, you will fly into our Pellston base and from there receive the remainder of your assignment."

"What about Todd Ramsey? He's the one who spent most of the time in that area. I've been exposed; I thought I was a permanent desk jockey," said Brooks.

"He's busy—plus he's a known entity there. I'm sure your exposure won't resonate in Michigan. You leave today. I suggest you get ready."

The other five members of the group never spoke. They watched the interactions, and as soon as the Chairperson gave her instructions, they left. She stood, staring at Mansfield and Brooks who were still seated.

"Thank you, ma'am. I'll see John gets to Langley as soon as possible," Mansfield said as he stood up, restacked his papers, and grabbed Brooks by the upper arm.

As soon as the two men left, she picked up the only phone in the room. "Sir, we have a man on the way. Yes, sir. Yes, sir. We'll keep it as close to the vest as possible. Thank you, Mr. President."

Sam was in her office at the computer, researching GRR and trying to find links to its ownership and board members. She knew its headquarters was located in Grand Rapids but they also had offices in several states and even overseas. Places like Spotted Horse, Wyoming (population twenty-three); Willston, North Dakota (population 20,000); and in Moscow, London, and Nigeria.

Sam pressed a speed dial number on her office phone. "Parker?"

"Hey, honey, what's up?"

"Got a minute?"

"Sure, just walking in for some coffee at Roast & Toast. I'll sit outside here a minute since the weather's warming."

"You ever been to Spotted Horse, Wyoming?"

Parker, who had been almost everywhere, laughed as he spoke. "You actually don't go to Spotted Horse. You drive through it in nanoseconds."

"That small?" Sam sat back, perplexed.

"It's only on the map for the post office."

"How about Willston, North Dakota?"

"Yup. Bigger but barren and windy."

"Why would an energy company from Grand Rapids be in those two places and now be attempting to locate in Frederic?"

"You want *The Grapes of Wrath* tangential and abstract soliloquy or the short answer?"

"What do you think?"

"Oil. Remember, money and power. People in those places have neither. Oil and gas gives them everything."

"Right." Sam looked back at her computer screen. "Why Moscow, London, and Nigeria?"

"Well, Russia is the largest producer of oil in the world. Nigeria has oil but lots of unrest. London? That would be banking."

"Banking?"

"During the 1990s and early 2000s, Wall Street moved a lot of its operations to London to get away from U.S. regulations and regulators, and then they got greedy. Thus the crash in 2008 and the Euro crisis today. Now those same banks control about fifty-six percent of all the wealth in the world."

"Need one to do the others?"

"You need to finance oil-and-gas research, development, and production. If not in London, then the Caymans, Hong Kong, or Singapore."

Sam went from screen to screen as Parker answered her questions. His propensity for long answers usually resulted in down time for her mind, but today his timing was perfect.

"Okay. Thanks, honey." She sat back again. "What have you been up to?"

"Um, nothing. Went and visited with Tim for a bit. Nothing special."

"All righty then. I'll see you for dinner—or before at the gym?"

"Gym. See you then."

Sam continued scanning Google find after Google find. An article from two years ago, referencing GRR, mentioned Pat Coruthers.

The old-timer's home was a ten-by-fifty 1958 Great Lakes trailer. It looked every year of its age. There were two bedrooms in the rear and a kitchen in the front. An old set of brown Naugahyde furniture; two end tables; and a large, dark brown coffee table filled the living area with more than just a musty odor. Throw rugs covered worn green linoleum, and a piece of dark green outdoor carpet over a plank of plywood covered a hole in the floor underneath the couch. There were dishes in the kitchen sink and crusty bread on a plate sitting on the small metal Formica table. Two metal diner chairs with yellow backs and seat covers split with age in several striations, as if a knife was used to cut them, sat just out from under the table. The 1960's Norge refrigerator with a pull handle that locked was filled with Busch Light beer and a half full bottle of Jim Beam whiskey. Some chewing tobacco pouches and tins of dip sat along the back of the side kitchen counter. The old-timer had guns in every room, including a 30-06 Springfield rifle with a well-worn walnut stock in the master bedroom.

The intruder picked up the rifle by its barrel with a gloved hand. He brought the stock to eye level and noticed lots of fingerprints, so he set it down carefully on the Naugahyde couch. He walked back out the side door and down the metal staircase. He looked up and down the side of the trailer and saw nothing but black spruce and tamarack surrounding it. The two-lane road that ended at the stairs was rutted with grass in the middle, and the drive back into the property was almost two miles, so the test well was about a half mile behind the trailer to the north of Cameron Bridge Road, another five miles from the closest residence in Deward.

Deward was a ghost town named for David E. Ward, who was one of the last great lumber barons. He owned virgin white pine forests that stretched from the middle of Michigan from Frederic and Vanderbilt over to Boyne City and East Jordan along Lake Charlevoix. Some of his holdings included land in the Upper Peninsula. The old-timer's plot was a remnant of his grandfather's land; his grandfather had worked for Ward at the turn of the century in 1901. There were as many as eight hundred people living in the area back then, when the post office was established. All that remained were the foundations of buildings, two-lane roads, and thousands of acres of state forest replanted around thousands of acres of massive white pine stumps. No one lived within five miles of the old-timer's white-and-green trailer.

The intruder who killed the old-timer the previous Sunday had been trying to buy him out for weeks, but the old-timer wanted more and more money and threatened to talk about the hidden test well north toward Lost Lake, one of the few lakes in the Lower Peninsula that didn't have a road leading to it. There was a two-track that existed only in good weather for a short period in the summer and fall. The test well was sunk without permits and without the knowledge of the township. Red tape was always a problem for GRR.

After strategically placing a few packages, the man in black slacks, new Johnston & Murphy shoes, and a black trench coat went back inside to make sure all was as it had been when he first entered the unlocked trailer. He grabbed the rifle off the couch, closed the door behind him, and made sure no footprints led to his trail into the forest. It was about a mile to his black Escalade that was parked on a dirt trail off Post Road.

The afternoon was turning to early evening.

ſ ſ ſ

John Brooks was packed and on a plane out of Langley. He wasn't sure of all the details, but he was sent well-armed and the vehicle he would pick up at Pellston Airport was bulletproof. The details he was given included an order to shoot on sight if necessary anyone connected to the Dubai super PAC, Resources For All, and associates of GRR who appeared threatening to the general public. The situation was obviously more serious than he had joked about in the briefing room. Frederic was about to make an appearance on the national map and he was supposed to contain the madness–or prevent it all together.

ſ ſ ſ

"So, how was the rest of your day?" Parker was walking on the treadmill next to Sam's at Center City Gym.

"Did you know that Patrick Coruthers owns most of the empty buildings on East Mitchell Street and Kathi's place is his first venture on Lake Street? He starts people off, raises their rent to the sky, then doesn't care if they have to vacate." Sam's eyes were riveted on Parker as he walked. Her affect was stern and her brows furrowed. "He uses the equity or assessed value for other investments. And, he's the President and CEO of Grand Rapids Resources, otherwise known as GRR, with offices and strategic centers in London, Moscow, Nigeria, Wyoming, North Dakota, and Michigan. He is a proponent of hydraulic fracturing for both oil and gas."

"Sounds like Kathi's got a future problem." Parker picked up the pace on his treadmill. "And I suspect you don't like the fracking thing?"

"It's bullshit." Sam began to run. "If I ever see that guy again, I'll make sure we have a discussion."

"Sam," Parker was keeping pace with her, "please tread easy. A guy in a business that big has people like us for breakfast. Let me do some snooping."

Sam jumped off the treadmill so that her feet straddled the moving belt. "You snoop; I snoop. We do this one together."

"Fair enough. Let's take a trip to Frederic tomorrow after my lunch appointment for John Stanley." Parker was giving most of his attention to the ballgame on the TV above him.

Sam jumped back on her treadmill. "You got it. Now, whadda ya wanna do for dinner tonight?"

Parker never took his eyes off the game. "You."

ť ť ť

"Painted Cottage, this is Kathi." Kathi was on the phone as she checked-out someone at the cash register.

"Mrs. Morris, this is Robert Clauson, attorney for GRR Holdings. Is this a good time?"

"Actually, no. I'm busy with a customer."

"Very good. I will be up sometime next week to see how things are going."

Kathi stammered as she attempted to help her customer while wondering why an attorney was coming to see how things were going. The call was not comfortable. "Sure, any day … but I really do have to go. Thank you."

Kathi hung up and gave her attention back to her customer. "I'm so sorry. Is there anything else I can get for you?" She tried to be calm, but the reward and self-gratification of the new store had suddenly disappeared into a mystery voice that essentially owned her.

ƒ ƒ ƒ

The black Escalade was parked in the same spot on Williams. Darkness had settled in after a perfect orange-and-red sunset over Little Traverse Bay. Only the slightest remnants of color remained on the horizon as Sam and Parker looked out from their bedroom window.

Picture after picture was frozen on the camera's screen waiting for the next one.

"Hope your flight was good. No change here. Ready for the next event," said the driver of the SUV into the vehicle's Bluetooth system.

ƒ ƒ ƒ

Down the street from the Escalade, in a ten-year-old, battered, gray, bulletproof Buick Regal sat John Brooks. He listened to the call from the SUV and noted the telephoto lens hoisted just outside the driver's window. On a hunch that his two friends might be involved, Brooks had decided to drive by Parker and Sam Moore's house to see if all was in order. When he drove by the suspicious Cadillac twice, he knew something wasn't right. He'd already called the plate number into Fort Meade. The vehicle was rented from a Hertz dealership in Grand Rapids; paid for with a GRR credit card.

Since this was no coincidence, John Brooks decided to park his car in a less conspicuous spot and wait until the Escalade moved. He parked around the corner on Bay Street and quietly but quickly exited the car.

His black clothing was an easy cover when he stayed on the back streets. Mitchell Street was well lit, so he avoided it. He walked behind the houses on Williams and watched the vehicle for several minutes. No change. The windows were blackened, but Brooks's earpiece connected to the directional microphone in his car allowed him to hear everything within the blackness.

He silently and methodically made his way behind the vehicle. In a second he attached a magnetic tracking device to the undercarriage without instigating any activity or response from the man behind the wheel. He could still hear the camera's shutter clicking.

After several more careful minutes, Brooks was back inside his Buick. He turned off the laser mic and turned on the computer which showed the location of the Escalade right where it should be. As he settled in and turned the ignition, the Escalade began moving. Left on Mitchell and past Parker's home. Brooks began following out of sight. He waited until the SUV drove past Division and out toward Wolverine before he even turned left onto Mitchell Street. As he passed the Moore residence he quietly waved.

"What the hell you into now, Moore?" Brooks said softly to himself.

ƒ ƒ ƒ

"Parker, you going to come away from that window?" Sam called from the stairwell as she looked up through the slats in the rail. "Come on, the movie's starting!" She ran back down.

"Yeah, yeah," Parker said in quiet preoccupation.

Parker first noticed the Escalade, then, just as he was turning to walk away from the window, he saw a gray Buick pull up to the stop sign on Williams and pause. He had taken two full steps away from the window but almost fell forward into the full-length glass when he recognized the beat-up Regal. He caught himself and froze.

*That's the same car that scrambled Stefanie's brains all over the pavement in Lansing three years ago.*

The incident was a distant memory, but any flash of familiarity brought the death of his abusive ex-wife to the front of Parker's thoughts. Like an addiction to nicotine or heroin, the recall was that quick–and that chilling. He could feel his palms begin to sweat and the hackles on the back of his neck stand up. He remembered that car. He tried not to change his stance and pretended to not be there. He was only a foot away from the sill.

He watched.

*Shit. NSA. What the hell is going on?*

"Parker, what the heck? It looks like you've seen a ghost."

Parker had walked slowly down the stairs as if in a trance. "No. I'm good. I'm good. Must be the chicken. I'll be fine," Parker said softly as he grabbed Sam and pulled her next to him on the sofa in the media room. *Bull Durham* played on the Blu-Ray. Parker stared straight ahead at the screen but never heard a word of the movie.

ƒ ƒ ƒ

The men, along with a smattering of women, milled around the pine-paneled great room. The nondescript log building sat a few yards off Old US-27, about ten miles north of Grayling, just inside the Frederic Township boundary. The sign out front was a simple coat of arms with no words. The Swamp, down the road, was empty except for a few drunks sitting at the bar telling old hunting stories.

"Gentlemen, ladies," the man at the front table tried to call the group to order. He leaned over to the man sitting next to him, "Sergeant? Could you get up and flick the lights to get everyone's attention?"

"Everyone! Please!" There was no mic, but the crowd was slowly coming to order. "Attention!" he yelled firmly and the crowd stood at attention in front of their seats. "I pledge allegiance to the flag …"

The group completed the Pledge and remained standing. "Sir, all members present and accounted for, except Mr. Gray."

"Thank you, Sergeant. At ease."

The group sat on tan metal chairs—two sections on both sides of a center aisle. There were thirty-two people in attendance, and many open carried .45 caliber Colt automatics.

"We've called this special meeting to ask for your help. Mr. Gray has been missing for several days and, if you know Dorian, you know that's not unusual, but Mr. Taylor drove by Gray's pickup over on 612 the other morning, and then went to Gray's home where he noticed some suspicious footprints bigger than Gray's. Also, Mr. Swanson spotted a black Escalade a mile or so from Dorian's trailer. So, with all of that, we'd like to organize some search parties tomorrow."

"Commander, our emergency plan has several groups designated for emergency functions. We can use those lists," the Sergeant noted.

"Very good. We'll assemble at the fire station at 8:00 a.m. sharp. Any questions?" the Commander asked as he stood with his sidearm in full view. "Fine. Unless there's any other business …" He paused. "We'll adjourn to the Swamp."

With that, six-foot, three-hundred-pound Commander Hal Morris of the Frederic Chapter of the Michigan Militia dismissed his group. The room emptied with loud banter and chairs banging as they were placed back onto the racks in the rear of the room. The walls contained hunting trophies, flyers for upcoming militia events, and a copy of the United States Constitution, Bill of Rights, and the Declaration of Independence. On the wall behind the front table was the famous flag of the

Green Mountain Boys of Vermont and the Gadsden flag with its snake and famous inscription *Don't Tread on Me.*

The militia members talked as they strolled to their cars parked along Old 27. There was no traffic on the late, chilly spring night.

"Hey, Commander," said the Sergeant following close behind. "When did you get the new truck?"

"Um, a few weeks ago." Commander Hal Morris stumbled on his words as he stopped momentarily to reply.

"Wow. Somebody die or something and leave you a bunch of money?" The Sergeant couldn't stop gazing at the shiny, new, midnight blue Ford F-250 with a waving American flag etched into the rear window.

"Don't be ridiculous. Got it at Grayling Ford. Now, Sergeant, I suggest you hightail it over to the Swamp and get started on the pitchers. We'll all be there sooner than later."

"Yes, sir," the Sergeant said as he ran over to his rusted-out, brown Chevy pickup.

Morris opened the door of his truck. A man wearing a black trench coat, black slacks, and Johnston & Murphy dress shoes was sitting in the passenger seat. Morris hesitated when he saw the unexpected rider with his arms folded.

"What are you doing in my truck?"

"*Your* truck?" replied the stranger as he watched Morris's large hands grasp the inside of the door frame. "I believe this is still a loaner."

"Not according to Mr. Coruthers. I earned this fair and square. A deal's a deal," Morris said shutting the door and situating himself in the bucket seat. He turned on the ignition and looked over at the smaller man.

"Well, it's yours as long as you continue to hold up your end of the bargain."

"Look, everyone in town was coming to me about Gray. I had to make some kind of effort."

"Just make it a small effort and in the wrong direction. Now, drop me off at the back part of the cemetery."

Morris turned his truck around and headed south, away from the Swamp and up the next drive into the cemetery. In the back of the one-hundred-year-old willowed property was a black Escalade. As the Johnston & Murphy's stepped down out of the pickup, they landed on the headstone of a grave. Thomas Moore, Veteran of the Army Signal

Corps. Born July 28, 1934; died September 27, 1997. Parker Moore's father.

Standing behind a grove of black spruce on the hillside, John Brooks watched the two trucks drive away.

*He looked up from his oil-drenched hands after his shift repairing wellheads and gazed across the Amu Darya and into Afghanistan. He dreamed of life before the Mujahedeen, the Russians, the Taliban, and the Americans. He missed his fields of poppy and wondered how the new saffron fields were doing as a replacement for the once famous, now infamous, opium trade. Wars that were fought over a beautiful plant and flower now began over black sludge and liquid gas.*

*Turkmenistan was no home. It was a refuge. He looked up and promised Allah that soon he would have an answer to end this carnage. The three other men working the wellhead said they had met a stranger who could arrange an end to the people who owned the wells and were smuggling his once prized opium into Turkmenistan, Uzbekistan, and Tajikistan for profits hidden in Moscow banks. Profits? While he and his wife and children slept on cots, they were hording profits?!*

# SIX

WEDNESDAY, APRIL 13

"PARKER? PARKER? YOU UP?" SAM WAS ALREADY PULLING the covers down and making the bed. Parker was still in it.

"Yes! I've been awake since the cats started to crawl all over my head." He didn't move.

Sam yanked the covers from around him.

"They're hungry. Get to it. We got places to go."

Parker sat up. Closed eyes and a mop of greasy hair greeted Sam.

"I'm up. I'm up," he said as he made his way out of the bedroom and down the hallway toward the bathroom. As he walked down the stairs to the kitchen both cats ran past him.

Sam yelled down, "Pack some stuff for a snack—and make coffee. Let's get outta here before I start getting work calls."

As Parker opened the cat food, shuffled coffee filters, the grinder, and the coffee pot around, he could plainly see the Escalade followed by the Buick in his mind. The slowness of the pass and the eeriness connected to his past life, made him angry it was all back. The time to find out more about Coruthers was now, and Sam's protection was the priority. In his preoccupation, he completely forgot about making the trip to Frederic a two-fold mission: land for John Stanley's project and Sam's anti-fracking crusade. Suddenly he felt more like a bodyguard. He almost wished he had his old 12 gauge shotgun, but Sam didn't allow guns in the house, and Parker figured he'd never need one again, so he had given it to his son-in-law.

"Honey?" Parker walked over to the stairwell and yelled upstairs. "Can we take a walk around the river in between visits today?"

Sam looked out of the bathroom at the top of the stairs. "Absolutely. I'll bring extra clothes." She was always excited to be in the woods.

"Great," Parker said softly as he dragged himself back into the kitchen. He picked up the empty plates after the cats were done, and let them outside. He stared at the same spot where a year ago the assassin was shot and died on his deck. "The NSA? I know where I'm startin' with this," he said confidently to himself.

ʄ ʄ ʄ

"Alright everybody, listen up." Hal Morris was acting like the militia Commander he was. "We're going to forget the grids we have previously assigned everyone, and check east of here toward Hartwick Pines."

There were about twenty people gathered. A USGS survey map of the area lay out on the open tailgate of his pickup truck with full cups of coffee on the corners holding it down.

"But Hal, we should go the other way, toward Kalkaska, where Gray kept his bait piles and anything else he wanted nobody to find," yelled someone from the back of the group.

"Shultz, I hear ya, but I got some information that he was headed out the opposite way in the days before he disappeared."

Morris turned back to the map and pointed to the other side of the Au Sable River and along a two-track between Lovells and Lewiston east of Hartwick Pines State Park. "Here, along this forest road toward Twin Lakes. We all know Gray liked a little elk meat. This would be a good place to start and work back toward Frederic. Now, here are your quadrants."

Morris began showing each team leader where to go and who to take. Each group grabbed radios since cell phone service was sketchy at best. Morris looked at his watch. It was just after 8:30 a.m.

ʄ ʄ ʄ

After finishing dinner, Sir Edward waved for the private waiter and bartender to remove the dishes and drinks. Pat Coruthers sat in one of the leather chairs next to Sir Edward's favorite sofa.

"A little tawny, Mr. Coruthers?"

"Please."

"Sergei, two ports. The good stuff."

"Sir," said Sergei as he slightly bowed behind Sir Edward.

"Now, where were we? Right. We've established a lobby office—I'm sorry, a consulting office, in Lansing, and have given you access to several people with experience in our most productive states."

"Yes, and I've been in contact. Since taking this position for GRR, I believe we've proven very successful for your group."

"Indeed. We have been very happy. The last debacle will not be repeated. Evgeny has indicated he has someone working with you for security of the project. Has all been smooth and up to your expectations?"

"Yes. He is a little dark, but very efficient."

"Dark?"

"I assume he had history."

"Right. According to Evgeny, these are professionals. Your person was educated at Columbia and held a diplomatic passport for years within the U.S."

"That will come in handy, I'm sure." Coruthers smiled confidently as he took his port from Sergei's tray.

Sergei walked over to Sir Edward and placed the tray in front of him so he could grab his own.

"Mr. Coruthers, where are we with the insurance policies?"

"I meet with our man on Saturday. The legal team is reviewing the binder now."

"GRR is the policy holder, correct?"

"Yes. There is no connection anywhere to RFA, and Lloyds of London will protect any loss, lawsuit, theft, or anything else you might imagine. They have been given the accounts in Hong Kong for payment upon acceptance. Our cover man from northern Michigan only knows that GRR is looking for protection on a normal piece of hunting property that may entertain high-profile clients. The Lloyds representative set up a temporary office in Grand Rapids and appeared very much like a local."

"Excellent. A toast then. To gas and profits."

The two clinked the Waterford crystal and looked out the windows as the sun set over the Persian Gulf.

# SEVEN

"WHERE DO WE START?" SAM WAS IN THE FRONT SEAT looking at a map. "Why is it you don't use a smart phone or GPS for directions or locations?"

"Why?" Parker returned the question as he drove them into Crawford County on County Road 612.

"So you don't get lost—and you know where you're going."

"Do I get lost or never know how to get somewhere?"

"No."

"So?"

"Okay. You're a human atlas. I'd feel better if I had something."

"So, we'll get you one."

"Good. Now, where do we start?"

"At the Swamp with a Bloody Mary."

"You're talking my language now! Can't you drive faster?"

ſ ſ ſ

John Brooks was staying at the Ramada Inn in Grayling under the cover name Joseph Granger, in town to survey floodplains. He walked down to the hotel's café for a late breakfast after a long night of driving and general "spook work" as he called it. His phone rang.

"Yes?"

It was John Mansfield in Fort Meade. "John, we have everything we can get on Grand Rapids Resources, and we have the vehicle marked from last night, but we need more than your description on the mystery man."

"K. I'll try to get some prints and pictures." Brooks looked out the window while he talked, ignoring the others in the restaurant.

"I wanted to let you know that the President is taking a personal interest in this."

"So, this is bigger than Frederic?"

"This may be bigger than all of us. Priority measures, got it?"

"Got it." Brooks put his phone in his pocket.

"Excuse me, is anyone using this chair?" a woman at a table next to Brooks asked.

"No. No, not at all. Please."

"Thank you." As she dragged the chair toward her, she bumped John's table and his coffee spilled in his lap.

"Shit!" he yelled as the hot liquid burned through his blue jeans and onto his left thigh.

"Oh, my! I'm so sorry." The woman grabbed a napkin and handed it to Brooks as he stood and tried wiping the coffee off his jeans.

"It's okay. I'm sorry I swore so loudly."

"Are you kidding? I used to swear like a truck driver. My son Parker told me to tone it down." She hesitated and looked around. "I'd have said a whole lot worse than shit."

Brooks smiled and suddenly caught the name of her son. "Did you say your son's name was Parker?"

"Yes. Parker Moore. Do you know him? He's not easy to miss. In fact," she looked around again, "his father used to say 'that was stacking shit pretty high,' since he's six foot five."

Brooks couldn't contain his laugh and he ended up spitting out the water he just sipped as he sat back down. "Oh, my god," he said all at once. "I am so sorry."

"So, you do know him?" Mrs. Moore sat down at Brooks's table since her party had yet to arrive.

"No. No, I don't! But I never heard a mother describe her son that way."

"Well, Parker has done a lot in his life, and most of it is a mystery to me. Everybody seems to know him though."

"Perhaps in the future. Now, if you'll excuse me. I really need to run." Brooks didn't want to spend any extended time around Mrs. Moore since his cover was important. He figured he'd better tell her who he was. "I'm Granger. Joseph Granger, in town surveying."

"Surveyor? Are you one of those assholes from FEMA looking

to raise our insurance rates on the river where there's never been a flood?"

He was caught off-guard by the fact she knew about the FEMA issue. "Um, well, I don't work for FEMA, but I am surveying some land up here around rivers and lakes for FEMA." Brooks was quick to recover and thought the whole FEMA thing could be valuable later.

"Well, I'm sorry for the spill," Mrs. Moore stood and looked toward the hostess approaching with two other women. "Ah, my guests are here. Good day, Mr., ah, Mr. …"

"Granger."

"Granger. Mr. Granger. Good luck with your surveys."

With that, Jackie Moore turned and sat down with her friends. John Brooks quickly made for the exit and out to the gray Buick Regal.

"God almighty. Of all the people to spill coffee on my pants. Shit!" he muttered to himself as he drove away.

"So, who was that young man?" asked Gretta who lived a few miles down the Manistee River from Jackie Moore. She was leaning down on her right side as she placed her large purse on the floor.

The waitress arrived to fill their coffee cups.

"Yes, who was that?" added Cynthia, Gretta's sister and another river neighbor.

"Oh, I don't know. Some FEMA asshole." Jackie Moore looked out the window as John Brooks drove away. Then she quietly added, "Glad I spilled the coffee."

"What was that?" Gretta asked leaning across the table as she adjusted her hearing aid.

"Nothing. Nothing." Jackie brought her attention back to the table. "So, where are we quilting today?"

Sam and Parker were on their second Bloody Marys. Parker was making notes in his journal while Sam read the local newspaper, the *Grayling Avalanche*.

"There's an op-ed about the meeting in Frederic Monday night. 'Mrs. Sam Moore appeared in front of Senator Dutch Van Der Knacht and a hostile crowd at the Frederic Township Hall …' Hostile? Jesus, they were downright rude."

"Mm hmm." Parker kept writing.

"There's more: 'The difficulty with the anti-fracking message of Mrs. Moore and her group is that the local people need the work that would be available within the framework of drilling and discovery, along with the sale and/or leasing of mineral rights as an income to local property owners. With an unemployment rate higher than fifty percent in this town of Libertarians, she picked a tough place to launch her argument.' That's an understatement. Parker are you listening?"

"Yes. Drilling. Launching." His eyes weren't diverted from his notes.

"I understand you have your business today, but I have to get ready for the next hearing in this very building."

"The Swamp?" Parker looked up. "Great. Now you'll have a drunk, hostile crowd. I would urge you to ask for a different venue."

"Can I do that?"

"Yes. They can decline, but you can talk about the alcohol factor. Get the local township supervisor involved."

"Parker, who do you think wrote the piece I was reading to you?"

"The township supervisor-reporter-editor person?"

"He's so pro-fracking it's pathetic."

"Then you're not doing the meeting alone. The alcohol can't run during a public meeting, but it doesn't stop them from before and after. Why here?"

"I don't know. Some conflict at the Township Hall. Fine. I'll call the rest of the group to go with me."

"Good. Look." Parker pointed at a poster hanging by the bar. "Mike Ridley's here the night of the meeting. That's a good thing. He's pro-fracking, but it makes me feel better he'll be with you."

Mike Ridley was a well-known Michigan troubadour and landowner from well north of Frederic in the Burt Lake area. His music was a favorite of the locals, and Sam and Parker had befriended him a few years ago while he was playing at the Noggin Room in Petoskey. Ridley would always let them know when he was coming to town.

"Mike must not know what he's in store for. He wouldn't play for an audience juiced up about fracking – for or against," Sam said thoughtfully.

"They'll be juiced up alright. You want me here?"

"No. I need to do this on my own."

"Okay, but I'll be awake until you get home."

A group of militia folks sat down at a table behind them for a round of coffee. "Any luck?" asked the Sergeant of the other four people.

"No," they all mumbled.

"Are you kidding me?" the Sergeant snapped back at them, then sat back in his chair and put his hands behind his head while re-thinking his anger. "Gray never did anything toward Lovells or Lewiston, and wouldn't be caught dead around a state park."

"Sure hope he turns up. Makes me nervous, him gone missing like that. He only goes missing when it's on purpose, and he usually lets someone know," added the only woman at the table looking into her cup as if the missing man would appear in the black liquid.

Parker couldn't help but overhear the banter. He leaned in close to Sam who was quietly cursing the rest of the op-ed.

"Hey?" he whispered. "Did you hear that?"

"What?"

"The talk behind us about some guy named Gray who's gone missing."

"No." Sam started to look behind her, but Parker grabbed her hand to stop her.

"Don't. Gray is the guy who helps my mom with her winter wood. An old Vietnam Ranger. They said he's missing."

"So? He's missing."

"Former Rangers don't get lost. Come on."

Parker dropped money on the table and started to lead Sam out of the Swamp. She had to reach behind her with a free hand to grab her sweater and the paper she was reading.

"Parker," she whispered in anger, "what the hell are you doing?"

They were outside heading toward the car when Parker looked up and spotted the Escalade and the driver smoking a cigarette behind the wheel. What he didn't see was the Buick Regal parked across the street at the BP station. Parker looked away quickly, but the driver continued to stare straight ahead as if he didn't care that he might have been noticed.

# EIGHT

PARKER AND SAM DROVE WEST ABOUT NINE MILES AND then turned north onto Manistee River Road. It was three weeks before trout season and two months before most of the vacation homes along the river would come to life; it was no-traffic time for Parker. He flew up the dirt road until making a right onto Cameron Bridge Road. All at once, he stopped.

"Parker? What the hell?" Sam had lurched forward and was picking up some papers previously lying on her lap.

Parker looked in the rearview mirror, waiting for the dust to clear.

Nothing.

He did several quick stops for another mile.

"Parker, goddamn it." Sam turned to look behind the car. "What?"

Parker was about to begin driving again, but Sam grabbed his hand off the wheel. "Honey, talk to me," she said softly, looking at him.

"There's been a black Escalade hanging around the house ever since you started the anti-fracking crusade. I think it's connected to that Pat Coruthers guy, and …" he paused to check the mirror again.

"And what?" Sam's eyes were bigger now and her whole body was turned toward Parker.

"And, it's the same kind of Escalade Coruthers drives—and I saw some old friends from the NSA tailing it the other night."

"Brooks? Ramsey? Who?" Sam's interest was peaking. She gaped at Parker and looked behind them.

"Not sure," Parker replied calmly and looked at Sam. "But it was the same car that killed Stefanie."

Sam turned and looked straight ahead out the windshield.

Silence.

"What do we do?" she finally asked in a calm voice.

"Trust me?"

"Yes."

"Now that I know we're not being followed, we'll go to Gray's and look around. Then I'll scope out the property for John Stanley, and call John Brooks. He won't be able to tell me anything, but if he doesn't answer or return the call, that will tell me a lot."

"After all that?"

"I may have to have my own personal conversation with Mr. Coruthers before I head to Washington."

"Washington?"

"Delivery for Stanley."

"So, um," Sam was sitting back in the front seat of the truck, quieter but stern. She looked at Parker. "When were you going to tell me all of this?"

"I wanted to get my facts straight." Parker was looking directly into her eyes. He had one arm draped over the steering wheel and a hand on the console between them. "When I saw the Escalade at the Swamp and the Buick, I knew everything was connected."

"Fracking?" Sam asked.

"Hydraulic fracturing," Parker replied as he glanced quickly out the rearview mirror before starting to drive again.

He drove a few miles down a two-track and stopped within sight of Gray's mobile home. No sign of cars or trucks after the overnight rain. Parker spotted a small camera mounted on a tree, and assumed it was one of Gray's wildlife cameras or a security camera for watching people who came near his trailer–like any good militia person would have.

The only sound they heard was the wind whistling through the pines and some chickadees.

# NINE

"GRAY?" PARKER YELLED OUTSIDE THE GREEN-AND-WHITE trailer. The screen door had been ripped and something, or someone, had been inside.

Silence.

Parker walked up the aluminum steps to the door and pointed to Sam to hold her spot on the first step until he walked inside. Sam sprinted up the stairs and into the trailer, bumping into Parker.

"That was subtle," Parker whispered to Sam.

"I'm new at this. We're a team, remember?" She looked up at Parker and held onto his waist.

The inside of the trailer was a mess. The place had been ransacked. Furniture was cut to shreds. Drawers pulled open. Food all over.

"Bears?" Sam asked.

"Maybe. The bear scat in the kitchen would say yes." Parker was laughing, but he knew this wasn't all bear.

They continued toward the back bedrooms. As they walked down the short hallway, Parker noticed wire and what looked like gray Play-dough in spots along the floor. As they reached the first bedroom, he smelled gasoline. Without hesitating, he grabbed Sam by the waist.

"Parker!" she yelled.

He hoisted her up under his right arm and kicked open the rear door. With a firm hold of Sam, Parker jumped from the top of the back steps onto the ground and tumbled forward. Sam rolled ahead of him. He got up, grabbed her around the waist, and carried her forward until her feet hit the ground, and she ran with Parker.

When the trailer exploded, they fell into the black spruce forest with Parker covering Sam. A huge fireball and thick smoke burst into the air; debris rained down everywhere. Parker stayed on top of Sam, her head buried in a muddy, damp mixture of pine needles and moss. A few pieces of insulation floated down around them; some landed on Parker's back. Aluminum siding clung to the branches above them.

In a few seconds, the sound was gone and so was the mobile home. All that remained was the steel frame and some smoldering pieces of what used to be someone's home. Papers continued to float down like a New York ticker-tape parade.

Sam forced her head up from under Parker's chest. As she spied the aftermath, she said, "Guess this was a bad idea."

The Escalade exited the parking lot of the Swamp and drove slowly toward Old US-27 which was the main road through Frederic. It turned south toward Grayling and M-72. The driver was still looking at the cell phone that dialed a number not expected to be picked up by a person. He smiled and put the phone down on the console next to the driver's seat.

After a few cars were behind the Escalade, the gray Buick followed. John Brooks was using his tracking device. He had no idea of what had just happened north of Frederic deep in the woods by the river.

# TEN

PARKER AND SAM WERE MOSTLY SILENT DURING THE hour-and-a-half drive back to Petoskey, and once inside the house, they both showered and were soon in bed. They didn't contact anyone about the incident, and Parker never completed his expedition onto the property he had located for John Stanley's factory.

Parker fell asleep quickly, but Sam couldn't relax. She went downstairs to the computer, and read article after article about fracking, including the one she'd found before that linked Pat Coruthers to GRR. Suddenly her laptop screen blipped, and Sam quickly took her hands away from the keyboard as if she had done something to it. Then, just as quickly, the screen seemed normal, so she continued to browse. There was, however, a slight slowness of speed that she didn't detect.

On the other side of the world, Evgeny watched Sam peruse material about GRR. As she read her emails to and from her friends in the anti-fracking crusade, so did Evgeny. He read along as she typed an email to the *Detroit Free Press*.

Evgeny grabbed his phone. "She's made the connection and is contacting the papers."

"Right. It is a public company. Why do you worry so, Evgeny?" Sir Edward seemed bothered.

"Our man says they've been snooping around parts of Michigan where we're becoming entrenched before all the leases, contracts, and insurances are complete. We should have waited."

"Nonsense. Where are they going to go to report such information? We have all of our money to the appropriate contacts, correct?"

"Yes," said Evgeny.

"Very well. She makes some noise, and we continue."

"Nonetheless I shall try to dissuade her."

"Do what you think, Evgeny. You have professionals on the ground protecting our interests. I shall also call the Michigan governor to assure he's taken care of. Good night, sir."

Evgeny didn't answer. He dialed another number. "They're still alive. I am watching her as she uses her computer."

"Okay. They're alive."

"Scare her–more."

"Very well, comrade. Allow me to finish this visit, and I shall have it done in the next forty-eight hours."

"Dos vedanya." Evgeny threw his phone on the sofa next to his desk and continued to watch Sam's computer.

John Brooks followed the Escalade all the way to Grand Rapids. It exited I-96 at 28th Street and proceeded west through Kentwood then south toward the airport. For most of the three-hour drive he stayed a mile behind the black SUV and simply used the monitor. As Brooks drove closer to the Escalade, he watched it pull into a private hangar area, park and wait until another black Escalade pulled alongside.

The stars were out, as Brooks waited and watched a man wearing a black trench coat step out of the vehicle and open the metal door of an old steel hangar and go inside. The light from inside was bright.

Brooks looked at his encrypted phone. The hangar was at an address belonging to GRR, and the plate he punched in for the other Escalade also belonged to GRR. His phone rang as he stared at the information.

"John, we've got some new intel on our Dubai folks. We have two calls between your GRR guys and a contact in Moscow. He's ex-GRU. Our group is looking to put this Dubai party back on our dashboard and getting rid of it once and for all. We have someone over there, so you need to keep on this and watch for a while. Clear?"

"Got it, chief. And Frederic?"

"It's all about gas and oil, John."

"Moore?"

"Got no clue yet how the hell he's involved."

"Maybe it's not him this time," Brooks said as he ended the call.

"Governor. Sir Edward here."

"Sir Edward, yes." The Governor of Michigan had fallen asleep after taking his nightly Ambien. "How are you?"

"I wanted you to know your retirement island is intact. I hope you enjoy it in a few years."

"Sir Edward, I'm not sure …"

"Nonsense. I won't hear of it. Please. No connections. No ramifications. Nothing necessary."

The governor felt his heart in his throat and could hear the pounding in his ears. He was pacing in the bedroom, his wife still asleep. *Was fracking this important? The leases were done and business was moving along as planned. Why this call?*

"Good-bye, governor. Enjoy your term and rest easy." Sir Edward was gone.

The governor put the phone down quietly on his wife's armoire as he stared into the darkness of the room–and his future. Suddenly, as if jolted by a shock, he grabbed the phone and erased the entry, even though he knew the call was still on record somewhere, even if the entry was titled Restricted.

Sir Edward pressed another button.

"Ingrid, did our payment reach the intended media markets in Michigan?"

"Yes. As did the rewards for the leases and votes. I have been told there will be over fifty people attending to make negative testimony. The good committee chair will gavel them dead. No comment will be held."

"How much?"

"All 56,954 square miles will be under our control."

"How much money?"

"Enough to make it happen."

"How many states now?"

"Twelve."

"Trail?"

"Never is."

"Takk." Sir Edward pushed a final button and sent a message to Evgeny:

**Call made. If we lose, take him quickly.**

*The masked man was always welcomed, although it took months to rid the group of suspicion. He was quiet, at first, allowing himself time to adapt and assimilate to the displaced Afghans. Once comfortable, the others found comfort in him. As was his new routine, he'd arrive with water and food as well as assorted treats for the children. The masked man was cognizant of what gifts were appropriate for the children. The tags always indicated a manufacturer within Islam, not the falseness of Turkmenistan. Trust may have been slow to arrive, but arrive it did.*

# ELEVEN

**THURSDAY, APRIL 14**

AFTER A LONG NIGHT ON THE COMPUTER, SAM WAS STILL asleep. Parker was in the kitchen when his phone rang.

"Good morning, Moore. Any luck on the property?"

"Working on it, John. Working on it." Parker popped the lid off the Friskies can while both cats stepped between his ankles, purring as they anxiously awaited their breakfast.

"What exactly does that mean?" barked John Stanley.

"It means I'm close." Parker's tone was flat.

John Stanley usually got what he wanted when he wanted it, and that was now; however, he sensed something in Parker's voice. Parker wasn't his usual positive self.

"Parker, I expect this to be done soon, so we can get on with the other parts of the plan. Architects, engineers, the whole nine yards." Stanley's voice softened.

"John." Parker paused as he tried to hold his anger. It wasn't John Stanley who'd blown up a trailer around Sam and him. "I found the area for the property. All in due course."

"I trust you, Moore. Sounds like maybe you had a helluva night. How about I buy today? Harbor. Bar Harbor. Let me know the time."

"Thanks, John. Yes. I will do *and* enjoy that."

"My love to Sam."

Parker watched the cats feast, then walked into the reading room and plopped on the loveseat. He sank into the cushion and thought about making coffee but didn't want to get up.

ϯ ϯ ϯ

In Fort Meade, the cadre of people the NSA had working on the new super PAC threat was growing. Anywhere there was fracking in the United States and abroad, the staff looked for connections to money and the politics—phone calls, texts, codes, emails, anything that might be related.

"Ma'am, we've got a hit from GRR. A number in Moscow. The same number we've found to and from London, Dubai, Azerbaijan, and Turkmenistan," said the young woman as she pointed at her computer screen while her supervisor looked over her shoulder.

"Got it. Mark it. Any details?" the supervisor asked as she started to walk away and pulled out her phone.

"I'm still trying to put all the messages together, but it sounds like they're watching a woman in Michigan and then something about a governor."

The supervisor, now sitting at a table behind the staff, gazed into monitors and screens while the many keyboards being touched made a rhythm she could tap her toes to. She took a breath and punched a number.

"Sir, we've got a hit in Michigan. I know we've got feet on the ground there …"

"And?" John Mansfield sat back in his chair and swiveled around to look out the window.

"Looks like a target."

"Uh-huh." Mansfield listened. "His mark?" He turned back to his desk and looked at his map.

"Affirm."

"John Brooks is there. Send him the notice, and keep me posted. Thanks, Evans. Good work."

"Yes, sir." Supervisor Evans beamed from the positive. Even though much of the NSA's work was done in the dungeons of computer rooms, they rarely had connections with field staff on the job, and rarely received direct compliments.

She sent the encrypted text.

ѓ ѓ ѓ

John Brooks sat in a coffee shop outside Plaza Towers on Fulton Street in Grand Rapids. He was watching and waiting. The Escalades had driven to this location during the night and parked in reserved spots right in front. In his tan khakis, blue oxford shirt with the sleeves rolled up, and a tie, Brooks looked like any other businessman having a morning break. He felt his phone vibrate.

His eyes widened as he read the text. He decided to check his office voicemail as well.

**John, Parker. I wonder if you've seen the spring snowpack up here? There's shit in it.**

Brooks knew exactly what Parker meant. Without directly asking Brooks if he was on assignment and where, Parker was letting John know he'd been spotted and Parker wanted Brooks to know they were on the same page. He smiled as he put his phone on the table and took a sip of coffee, looking over at the two SUVs—at least the somewhat relieved NSA agent knew who the target of protection was, and that the two men connected to the black Escalades were definitely the bad guys.

He was a card-carrying member of the NRA who believed Stand Your Ground laws were too soft. His .40 caliber Smith & Wesson was always concealed—and he didn't care who cared. The new house on Mullet Lake was his pride and joy. Protection was a must after his life spent in urban areas taught him there were always threats, and he especially knew the risks since his business was selling risk aversion. The insurance business was very profitable.

"Samuals," he answered his phone as he sat in his home office that overlooked the lake.

"Are we set?"

"Policies are ready, and you'll be protected," Dan Samuals said.

"For everything?"

"Even if the Mayans are correct," he said with a smile as he leaned back in the soft leather chair.

"Next week?"

"How about Chandler's?" Samuals placed the phone on speaker and checked his calendar. "Friday evening?"

"How much?"

"You sign that night, the whole premium."

"Thanks. Friday then. I'll call with the time." Pat Coruthers placed his phone down on his desk and turned his attention to his guest.

ſ ſ ſ

Parker sat in the chaise lounge in their bedroom looking at the city of Petoskey and Little Traverse Bay. To pass the time, he grabbed a book of Shakespeare off the shelf and read some of his favorite lines. He was upset at himself for disregarding the cameras he'd seen around Gray's trailer and placing Sam in harm's way. The deep blue of the lake took his mind away from the explosion momentarily. He looked across to Harbor Point and John Stanley's environs—some of the most beautiful coastline in the USA. From Petoskey to Mackinaw, Emmet County encompassed stretches of sand, rock, birch forest, and million-dollar homes. The water along the shore of the county and through the Straits of Mackinac was pristine. In fact, because of the invasive zebra mussels, the clarity of the water had improved–a good effect for tourists, but a bad effect for lake life. Parker returned to his book. Sam was finishing in the shower, having called her secretary to inform her she would be late to the office.

"Hey, what are you still doing here, my bomb-shield man?" Sam's question and humor took a little edge off the experience from yesterday.

"You know that trailer was rigged to blow?"

"That's what you've said. Gray was a Ranger and good militia member; maybe he had it that way."

"The bear would have set it off. No it was set after," said Parker.

"Coruthers again?"

"That's my guess."

Wrapped in a towel, Sam knelt down next to Parker and gazed out at the lake. "Isn't it gorgeous? Look where we live."

"I know," he said with a pause. "I know. I'm going across the bay to meet John Stanley later."

"Why would anyone want to muck this up?"

"The lakes? Let's see, money, commerce, energy, oh, and did I say money?" he remembered the zebra mussels and smiled. "If you're a true capitalist, the water is fodder for growth." Parker was rubbing Sam's back.

"Hmm. That feels so good." Sam stood up. "I'm doing my part to save that water." She dropped her towel and began to dress in front of the full-length mirror.

"Getting naked in public would help."

"No. I'm saving that for the next hearing I attend. Whaddya think, a striptease?"

"Absolutely."

# TWELVE

PARKER WAITED FOR JOHN STANLEY AT THE BAR HARBOR bar. Warm and sunny for mid-April, the snow from earlier in the week was now only in pictures. The harbor remained empty, but the guys at Irish Boat Shop and Walstrom Marina were busy getting boats ready in the shops and storage facilities around Harbor Springs.

The town was as quiet as the harbor and shoreline. The bar had a couple tables of locals in for burgers, beer, and pool. Parker sat in a booth by the entrance and waited for Stanley, but Sam was on his mind more than Stanley's legacy project. Something was amiss. *Hamlet's father lurked behind the mist in a black Escalade, while Lear's children plotted somewhere in Grand Rapids. Now, Henry's army waited for the next move. Whoa, too much Shakespeare*, he thought.

*Everything that was a threat pointed to Sam's work around fracking. Or did it? Was there a connection to the legacy project? It was in the same area. It was something that might create consternation in local folks not wanting it, but how would they even know about it? Sam was in danger.* That was cemented in his head. He didn't feel like it was his safety he had to worry about, but now that he was back on the grid, who knew? *Coruthers. He's a bad guy.* That thought just kept repeating itself over and over in Parker's head.

"Parker. Sorry I'm late, old boy."

In his preoccupation, Parker hadn't seen or heard John Stanley walk up to him. He immediately knew if he was to protect Sam, he'd have to be better at protecting himself.

"No problem, John." Parker stood out of the booth and shook hands with the impeccably dressed billionaire.

"I see you still dress like a flop."

"Always undercover for you, John." Parker looked himself over in his jeans and tweed sport coat. "John," Parker looked around and put his head close to Stanley's left ear, "I have holes in my underwear too," he whispered.

"Sit down and shut up!" Stanley said loudly, laughing and slapping Parker's back with his left hand. The other patrons looked over momentarily.

"The usual, Hannah!" Stanley yelled over his shoulder toward the bar.

"Oban, Parker?" she yelled back.

"No. Umm, you buying, John?"

"Lagavulin, Hanna," yelled Stanley.

"Thanks, John."

Hannah was already making John Stanley's martini as she reached over and grabbed the single malt.

"So, Moore, you look like shit. Tough night?"

"That bad? I thought I cleaned up better than that."

"Anything I can help with?"

"No."

"Sam?"

"Not sure. Let's just say I'm watching both sides of the street."

"You found property?"

"Yes." Parker paused as Hannah placed the drinks in front of the two men. "Thanks, Hannah."

John just nodded at her and continued the inquisition.

"Enough land?"

"Yes. Good, central location. Expressway access. Rail access north and south. Possible east and west depending on the money you sink in."

"Employees?"

"Ripe. About fifty percent unemployment in the area. Some on purpose, but the vast majority would rather work."

"Problems?"

"Probably."

"Money take care of it?" Stanley sipped his martini.

"I don't think so." Parker swirled his scotch in the snifter.

"You're joking, right?"

"No. I think there might be some serious shit, John. Anywhere you're competing with land that's being fracked ... some people know about it, some not."

"What can I do?"

"Not sure, yet. I'm prioritizing Sam, but I'll make that trip to D.C. for you, and I'll get my two local contacts working the inside. Hopefully you'll be building once the mud season is over." Parker sipped his scotch and leaned across the table to get closer to Stanley. "I assume you have the governor on your side?"

"He was, but you know, he's been jumpy lately. Not like him. He's usually very calm and purposeful in his mannerisms and work." Stanley sipped the last of his martini and put the glass down. "I wonder …" He looked out the window.

"John, there is nothing but good in this idea. It's a win-win for the state, for the people, and even the politicos."

John Stanley was intent on leaving this world with a legacy in the forefront of everyone's mind. He looked over at the bar and raised his glass toward Hannah. "Hannah, no olives this time."

"Parker, another?"

"No thanks, Hannah. I'm good." Parker could sense something in the recesses of his friend's mind. He watched Stanley take a slip of paper from his shirt pocket. He handed it to Parker.

"I know who your problem is. Wasn't sure until this meeting. He called the other day looking for a new American partner. I'm sure you'll find this handy."

Parker Moore was dumbfounded. He looked up in disbelief. The final piece of the puzzle. *King Richard had joined the fray.* The name scribbled on the paper:

***Sir Edward Framingham***

Parker sat back in the booth, seething, as John Stanley stood.

"How did …" Parker stammered.

"I have a lot of money, Parker. There's a lot of life around me you don't know about, but I know all about you. You're welcome. And call me when we can go public. I'll take care of the governor."

Stanley walked toward the bar. Hannah had her back to him. Parker looked out the window at the empty harbor. His anger welled; he couldn't wait any longer for John Brooks.

"What's the damage, Hannah?"

John Stanley downed his martini as soon as Hannah handed it to him, paid the tab, and left Parker stewing, but he knew the difficulty was in good hands.

# THIRTEEN

PAT CORUTHERS SAT IN HIS OFFICE ON FULTON STREET in Grand Rapids, looking out the window, with his Bluetooth on, and his iPad in his lap. He punched some numbers into a spreadsheet and smiled. He turned, stood, and walked over to the sofa in his elaborate office. Gifts and trinkets from all over the world filled the shelves. Anywhere he did business, he brought something back that signified the area.

"We're set. Thanks," he said. As he removed the Bluetooth from his ear and set it on the mahogany coffee table from Brazil, he looked at his guest and said, "That thing is necessary but it's a pain in the ass.

"What's next, Mr. C?" asked Dimitri Anakova.

"Nothing. Let's see what plays. The more we draw attention to this the more we have to worry about. The governor is bought and paid for by the PAC, along with appropriate committee chairs. She's dead in the water trying to fight this, especially since it's been going on for years. The other anti-fracking groups have been meeting around the state and can't make a dent."

"I know her schedule and can make her re-think her venture whenever you'd like." Anakova's English was better than his boss's.

"Stay close and enjoy yourself in the north, but keep quiet. We have some other holdings up there to ensure the public sees us in a positive light by *helping* business. Our attorneys and I will be up north soon." Pat Coruthers was the picture of confidence.

"Okay. I'll head back and do as you suggest, sir." Dimitri Anakova stood and helped himself to some vodka on the sidebar. No ice and no mixer. He was born in Moscow and a believer in the old ways—third generation GRU. His paternal great-grandfather was a Stalin colleague, and his paternal grandfather sent Dimitri away to Columbia University for his education and preparation for foreign service. After all, a relative of Leon Trotsky would do well—even in the new Russia. Dimitri listened to Pat Coruthers, but he knew what he did best. Sitting in the background wasn't what Evgeny was paying Dimitri for.

"Dimitri, please. Be patient. America is different."

"Mr. C, I've been working in America longer than I lived in Russia. I think I understand." Dimitri Anakova slammed his vodka. Slammed another, and walked out with a wave of his hand toward Pat Coruthers. "See you soon." Then he mumbled to himself, "Don't tell me how to do my job."

ˆ ˆ ˆ

John Brooks watched the black trench coat exit the Fulton Street high-rise and get into one of the Escalades. Brooks was relieved it was the SUV with the tracking device. The Escalade pulled out and headed for US-131 north. Brooks's plan was to snoop around GRR a little, then catch up with the SUV. In case headquarters had a different idea, he sent pictures of the trench coat to Fort Meade. Brooks never used local intelligence offices for information. First of all, because he wasn't directed to, but mostly because he believed local people would somehow tip-off the people he was surveying.

The response to photos of the trench coat was almost instantaneous:

> **Dimitri Anakova. Russian. Educated USA: Columbia University, NYC. Former GRU and Foreign Service. Private security for unknown company. Not found anywhere in GRR database.**

"Well, now. That's a lot of person for Petoskey!" John Brooks whispered to himself. He looked at his phone to follow Anakova's path. "Serious money brings serious security."

He thought quietly for a few minutes. His orders were clear, and he had the power over life and death on the street. The reply to Parker Moore may have to come sooner rather than later, especially with Sam involved. *This has to be our boys in Dubai.*

Brooks stood up, put on his sport coat, and ordered a coffee to go. As he turned, Pat Coruthers was getting into the other Escalade. *It might be interesting to see where he goes,* Brooks thought as he made his way to the Buick. Before opening the door, he noticed the parking ticket on the windshield.

"Shit. This doesn't happen to James Bond," he said as he laughed and yanked the ticket from the windshield.

ť ť ť

Anakova drove north on US-131 checking the screen mounted in the dashboard for messages from Evgeny. Nothing. He looked in his mirrors often and noted nothing suspicious. He was more lax in the Midwest. His narcissism and confidence told him he was in control.

ť ť ť

Sam Moore was in her office finishing lunch and listening to people in the boardroom across the hall. Her preoccupation with almost being blown sky-high wouldn't leave. She only had a couple more meetings this afternoon and thought about leaving early to prepare for tomorrow's hearings in Lansing. Although her business was health care, her passion was the environment.

ť ť ť

"Hey, you guys up for a simple dinner at the deli?" Parker said into the phone as he drove from Harbor Springs.

"Sure. I'll call Lance and make sure he's available," answered Rance Hennessey.

"Good. I'll count on it and be there at five."

"See ya, Parker."

ť ť ť

John Brooks frequently glanced at his phone to make sure Anakova was where he was supposed to be while he tailed Coruthers into an upscale neighborhood in Kentwood, and turned into a long driveway. The front of the house was partially hidden by a long hedgerow. Figuring the security of the grounds was probably advanced, Brooks kept driving. He also knew the Buick would be conspicuous in this neighborhood, so he made a mental note of the house details and street since no address was apparent. Just as he headed back toward 28th Street his phone vibrated:

**Latest text from Moscow to your mark: "Scare her."**

*Sam*! He pulled into traffic and sped toward I-96, and took the US-131 north exit. He needed to catch the other Escalade.

ɾ́ ɾ́ ɾ́

Anakova smiled as he read the message on his dashboard. *The old ways*, he thought. He pushed a tune into his phone and placed an earpiece in. Nikolai Andreyevich Rimsky-Korsakov's *Scheherazade* played softly as he drove north. His late afternoon and evening would be fun.

ɾ́ ɾ́ ɾ́

Pat Coruthers sat in his study at home having a late lunch with his wife when his Bluetooth noted a call.

"Yes?"

"Mr. Coruthers, I'm on my way to Petoskey to check the properties as you asked." It was junior attorney Robert Clauson.

"Good. Good. I've decided not to go, so make sure they meet you and get a positive feeling. You will be their contact from now on."

"No problem, Mr. Coruthers. I'll call you soon with the details."

"Very good, Clauson. We'll talk." He turned off the Bluetooth.

"Who was that, honey?" asked his wife as she settled her feet up on the Queen Anne leather recliner.

"One of our attorneys looking after our properties in the north."

"I should go shopping up there. It's been years," she said as a personal assistant delivered her a drink.

"Let's. I'll arrange a nice night for us at our Bay Harbor cottage." Coruthers thought maybe it would be nice to mix business with a little pleasure after he finalized the insurance matters.

ɾ́ ɾ́ ɾ́

It was almost 5:00 p.m. when Sam realized she'd actually been able to concentrate at work, but she was ready to leave. She walked out of the office building with some of her staff. They all said their good-byes and then began to pull out of the parking lot.

Anakova had timed his entry into Petoskey superbly. He was stopped in the right-hand turn lane at the light at US-131 and Lears Road as Sam Moore drove east through the light right in front of him. Little variance in her routine allowed his experience in this business to win. *Game on*, he thought in his best English. Anakova never thought in Russian while on the job. Too risky.

ꞙ ꞙ ꞙ

"Roast beef, ah, lettuce and tomato, mayo, and um, cheddar. Thanks, Jean." said Lance Hennessey as he ordered from the board above the counter at Harborside Deli.

"I'll have the same," Parker said.

Lance walked over to the table and sat with his brother Rance Hennessey while Parker went to the soda fountain to fill his cup with Coke. Parker joined Rance and Lance, sitting on the other side of the table from the brothers. The drive-home-from-work crowd was just beginning to roll in at 5:00 p.m. as sunlight streamed in the windows on the southwest side of the building.

ꞙ ꞙ ꞙ

At the first stop sign at Howard, Sam looked right and left before turning left. Out of the corner of her eye, she spotted the Escalade behind her. She felt her heart jump. She remembered what Parker had told her; she picked up her phone. Her mouth turned dry as the Escalade followed. She was trembling as the phone dialed Parker's number. She was already at the next stop sign. She dropped the phone, grabbed the wheel with both hands, and put both feet on the brake. The crowded intersection awaited her stop. As her car lurched forward, the phone slid under the seat. She tried to reach it but couldn't. The black vehicle behind her was so close it was all she could see in the rearview mirror.

Sam composed herself and let the intersection clear. She accelerated. Her glances in the mirror were with darting eyes; never moving her head. She smiled, turned on the CD, and began to sing along with Tracy Chapman—all in a ruse to act relaxed—since her heart was racing.

Anakova remained stoic. His earpiece was off, as the Bose 5.1 Surround Sound system continued with music blaring—Stravinsky. His blonde hair was cut perfectly, blown back and feathered over his temples and ears.

Sam reached another stop sign. This time she was prepared and stopped slowly. The Escalade kept pace and again blocked her mirror. All she could see was the chrome grill. She then accelerated quickly and stopped in hopes the phone would slide out from under the seat and magically appear below, but to no avail. All she heard was a clunk—the phone was stuck under the seat rail.

The Escalade bumped her back bumper, and the driver's door opened. Just as Sam saw a leg exit, she accelerated and eventually turned right onto Jennings. The leg slowly re-entered the SUV and Anakova proceeded north on Emmet Street.

Sam looked in her mirror and took a loud, deep breath. She sat back in her seat; shoulders rounded as she slumped. The phone was forgotten. Halfway to Kalamazoo, she made a left onto Lockwood. As she came to the stop sign at Grove, the Escalade was waiting.

Anakova didn't move. Stravinsky continued. He watched and waited. No expression. He'd run this game hundreds of times all over the world. This was easy. He brought a cigarette to his lips and lit it. He waited.

Sam punched the accelerator. She heard the phone clunk again.

"Shit!" she yelled; her eyes welled with tears.

The Escalade proceeded through but did not follow.

No deep breath this time for Sam. She pulled up a driveway, made sure the SUV was nowhere in sight, and got out of the car to reach under the front seat. She grabbed the phone, hopped back inside, and punched Parker's number–nothing but his voicemail.

"Goddamn him keeping that fucking phone off!"

She almost threw the phone in frustration, but on second thought, placed it next to her on the seat. She closed her eyes and breathed. When she opened her eyes and looked in the rearview mirror to back up, the Escalade was blocking her way. Without hesitation, she drove across the front lawn of the house she'd pulled up to and onto Lockwood, racing toward the alley behind her home. Sam looked in the mirror. The black

SUV had not moved. Way beyond worrying about unnoticed glances, she kept yanking her head back to look. “Sonovabitch. You get in my way again, I’ll fucking run into you.”

She flew down the alley at 50 mph, hitting tree branches and scraping a fence before pulling into her driveway. She had pushed the button to open the garage door on her approach, but had to wait until it opened enough for her to drive in, still, she bumped the bottom of the door with the top of her little Honda SUV. Before the door was all the way up, she hit the button to close it. She opened the side door of the garage and ran into the house through the back door. She slammed it behind her and ran to the front of the house to lock the front door and stopped.

She saw three Petoskey blue-and-whites surrounding the Escalade. One of the cars was balanced over the middle of the median on Mitchell. A blonde man in a black trench coat was face down on the pavement with two officers holding their guns on him. A half a block away to the right, she saw the Buick. One man inside.

Director Tim Johnson drove up the wrong way on Mitchell and parked his car facing the Escalade. He opened the door then kicked it open the rest of the way. His tan trench coat flopped in the breeze. Sam watched him walk up to the man on the ground and bend down over him. When he stood up, he told his men to take the man away.

Anakova cooperated with every step. He looked like the calm, cool spook that he was. He was cuffed and went into the back of the police car without a struggle.

Johnson waited for the patrol vehicles to leave before he looked around, and in an inconspicuous fashion pointed and nodded at Brooks. He then walked up to Sam’s door. She was peering out the window, but from the middle of the front parlor with the lights out.

“Sam! It’s me. Tim.” He looked and waited.

Sam was still. She couldn’t move. She brought her right hand up to her face and began weeping. Tim Johnson opened the door, and her weeping turned into sobs. Johnson walked slowly over to Sam and hugged her; she buried her face in Johnson’s chest, slumping in his arms.

“Do you guys ever get sick of the jokes about your names?” Parker asked, sipping his Coke.

"No," Lance said looking at Rance.

"Actually brings us more business," Rance responded, looking at Parker. "The more fun people have with our names, the better they remember us."

The two brothers were partners in Hennessey and Associates, a consulting firm with no specialty except to make connections and provide for the general welfare of their well-heeled clients. In fact, Rance and Lance were the best mouthpieces in town. From Petoskey and Harbor Springs all the way to the middle of the state, they could make anything happen—for a price. As consultant lobbyists, they were more like literary agents in the new millennium of publishing, i.e., they only took sure things.

"So, what gives, Parker? You make things happen for people all the time. Why us?" Lance was working on his roast beef sandwich.

"Yeah, Moore. Why us?" Rance echoed.

"I need some local help," Parker said as he took a bite of his sandwich.

"For?" asked Lance.

"A factory." Parker's mouth was full, so *factory* sounded like *actory*.

"A factory?" Rance looked at Lance.

"A factory?" Lance said, laughing.

"Are you on drugs? This is Michigan. Not just Michigan, but butt-fuck out-in-the-woods Michigan." Rance was leaning over the table with his neck stretched out as he looked at Parker.

"Whoa! Tell me what you really think!" Parker said as he leaned toward Rance and put only an inch between their noses.

"Okay, hold it boys. Let's just say you're not on drugs, Moore … where and for what?" Lance laughed as he reached for a French fry.

"Well, clothing. Over near Frederic." Parker took a bite of his sandwich and tomato and mayo oozed out the side.

"Frederic? FREDERIC!?" Rance laughed as he sat back in disbelief.

"Okay. He really is high," Lance said as he looked at Rance. "He is a crazy motherfucker."

Parker continued to listen as the men traded barbs. He was always amazed at the world of politicos, lobbyists, and consultants. Their language was always as coarse as that heard inside a hockey locker room, and the thought of new ideas absurd.

"Frederic," Parker nodded as he caught the back half of his sandwich squirting out from between the bread.

"Please, let us explore this idea, brother, with the utmost civility and due diligence. After all, Mr. Moore did buy us dinner." Lance did all he could to sound like the sophisticate. He sat straight and tall, and used his best East Coast Roosevelt accent.

"Bully. Bully. Yes, let's." Rance replied. He carefully placed his folded hands on the table and waited in silence.

Parker put his elbows on the table, clasped his hands under his face, and rested his chin on his left index finger. "I have a client who can invest whatever it takes to make it work."

"Materials?" asked Lance.

"By rail, from Lake Michigan or Huron."

"No east-west line. Only north-south."

"He'll build one," said Parker.

The brothers were taking turns asking details.

"Workforce?" Rance asked.

"Local and recruited if needed."

"Product?" Lance asked.

"Clothes. Shirts. Pants. Socks. Working man stuff. Made in America," Parker answered looking back and forth between the two brothers like he was at a tennis match.

"Cooperation and clearances?" said Rance.

"That's where you two come in."

"You can't afford us," said Lance.

"He can."

"He who?" said Rance.

"John Stanley."

"Stanley. John Stanley?"

"Harbor Springs' John Stanley?"

Rance and Lance were suddenly interested. The two brothers in their open-collared dress shirts, gabardine slacks, and penny loafers with no socks sat back and silently reacted.

"Look," Parker broke the silence, "we've set up a super PAC, and the first check will be delivered to D.C. for the federal piece. There's lots of space, and no one in this state is going to say no, but to be safe, you guys need to guarantee that for me."

"You talking utilities, environmental allowances, and everything that goes with it?" Rance asked.

"Yes."

"Shouldn't be too hard," Lance said, nodding to his brother.

The deli's late crowd was now thinning. Jean, the owner, walked over from behind the counter and stood behind the Hennessey brothers. "You guys need anything else? We're getting ready to close."

"No thanks, Jean. I think we're about done here," Parker said, smiling up at the woman. He smiled at Rance and Lance as they sat back in their chairs. Lance had his hands clasped and resting on his head, while Rance had his arms folded and resting on his belly. Both were staring at Parker. The surprised expression remained on their faces.

† † †

"Where's Parker?" he asked as he looked over Sam's head around the rooms behind her. He felt his weapon on his belt for comfort.

"I don't know. What the hell happened?" Sam backed away and looked up while wiping her eyes.

"We got a call and got here as soon as we could."

"Who called?"

Johnson knew but couldn't tell Sam—at least not now. "Ah, some neighbor reported a suspicious vehicle."

"Who is he? Wait. I know who he is. He works for GRR. That Coruthers asshole."

"Sam," Johnson held her by the shoulders and pushed himself back to look down into her eyes. "We'll figure it out."

Early evening sunlight streaked through the bay windows of the parlor as the sun slowly set while the days lengthened. Sam walked past Johnson, stood at the front door, and looked outside. "This isn't going to end well. If Parker, when Parker, hears about this, there's going to be hell to pay." She turned back toward Johnson. She was composed but angry. "What will you do with this guy?"

"We'll try to scare him. We'll try to keep him until we know something, but I got a feeling, he'll be out of my station in a short while." Johnson wasn't sure if John Brooks was going to talk with the man tonight or not. "Sam, I gotta get back. Are you alright?"

Before Sam could answer, they both heard the back door open. Johnson quickly pulled his Glock from its holster and held it along his right leg.

"Sam? Sam you home?" It was Parker.

"In here, Moore," answered Tim.

"Johnson, what the hell you doing here? Sam, you alright?"

She walked quickly to Parker, hugged him, and then backed away. "Where the fuck were you? Why don't you ever leave your fucking phone on?" Sam was distraught as the entire episode hit her. She was safe to yell—at everyone.

Parker was startled. He and Sam rarely shared a cross word. He looked over Sam at Johnson who was re-holstering his weapon. Johnson motioned to Parker with his eyes and a nod to follow him into the kitchen. He also put both hands out and placed his palms down gesturing for Parker to stay calm.

"I was taking care of some business, Sam," was all Parker could muster. He was still stunned by her outburst.

"Well, now you need to take care of me," Sam cried as she ran up the stairs.

"What the hell, Tim?" Parker looked like a deer caught in headlights.

"We'll talk later. Go take care of Sam. Everything is okay now." Johnson walked out the front door.

# FOURTEEN

ANAKOVA QUIETLY RODE TO THE PETOSKEY DEPARTMENT of Public Safety, quietly walked in with a police officer on either side of him, and then quietly sat in the holding room. His affect never changed. His hair was unruffled; his black shirt, slacks, and Johnston & Murphy's were neat and clean; and his trench coat was without a wrinkle.

Three officers waited for their boss, Tim Johnson, to return to the station. As they drank their coffee around the front desk, the GRR attorney walked through the front door. He had received an emergency call from Pat Coruthers.

"Excuse me. Robert Clauson, attorney for Mr. Anakova."

"Sure. Have a seat," one of the officers said, motioning to a chair behind the attorney.

Another officer retreated into the Director's office. "Chief," he said into the phone, "the mouthpiece for the perp is here."

"K. Just stay in the back office. I'll be there in five."

The officer closed the door before he set the handset on the receiver. Once the door was shut, he took a deep breath, sat down, and looked at his watch.

Clauson stood erect in his olive-green Armani suit. He held his briefcase in front of him with both hands grasping the handle. "Excuse me. What is the delay?" he said politely as he leaned ever so slightly forward.

"Ah, let me go check. I'll be right back," said the second officer as he walked back to the closed door. When he opened the door, he found the first officer sitting in the director's chair with his feet up on the desk. "What the hell?"

"The chief said to wait."

The door blew wide open and in walked Tim Johnson. He said

nothing, threw his trench coat onto the hook on the back of the door, then turned and walked out, slamming the door behind him.

"Can we help you, sir?" Johnson barked as he walked toward the front. He was in a mood to accost the attorney, but settled down and smiled as he finalized his approach to the front desk.

"Yes. Director Johnson," the lawyer put his right hand out, "my name is Robert Clauson."

Johnson shook his hand and took the lawyer's card. He didn't look at it.

"Back here." Johnson motioned with his head for Clauson to follow him. He did.

The two entered the holding room and sat at the conference table with Anakova. The other officers were gathered again by the front counter. Before they went back out on patrol, they watched the monitor for a few minutes. Anakova was sitting quietly with his hands cuffed through the recessed retaining bar atop the table.

"Mr. Anakova and Mr. Clauson," Johnson started as he sat across from the two men. "I'd like to make it clear that terrorizing my citizens will not be tolerated." Johnson was stern and angry, yet controlled. He knew he'd probably never see either of them again after this episode, so he wanted to make the best of it.

"Director Johnson, could you tell us who called in the complaint?" Clauson was not a true litigator, and certainly not used to this type of assignment. He was trying to take control. "I will go through appropriate channels, if necessary."

"No need for channels. It was anonymous from a blocked cell phone. You may proceed to find that out if you choose, but that is what you'll find."

Johnson and Clauson maintained eye contact and sat with their hands relaxed, on the table. Anakova looked at each man who was speaking as if he was watching a tennis match.

"Anything further, Director?"

Tim Johnson knew how this would end up. He wasn't going to spend a lot of time to make a point that wouldn't be listened to anyway. These guys were smooth, monied, and he was positive Anakova was dangerous—cold and dangerous. "No. We should be good." Johnson caught himself. "Before you go, Mr. Anakova, what interest do you have with Mrs. Moore?"

"Mrs. Moore?" Anakova broke a smile and acted confused as he looked at Clauson and then back to Johnson. “I don’t know a Mrs. Moore.”

“The woman you were terrorizing with your vehicle and curious driving habits.” Johnson pressed so Anakova would know that the Petoskey PD knew more than he thought.

“I’m sorry, Director. I was …” Anakova was interrupted by Clauson.

“Mr. Anakova, you don’t have to answer that, please.”

Johnson thought quickly. He wondered about making a point to tell Anakova that he was messing with the wrong husband, but he held the thought. The NSA and who knows who else was watching these guys; they were already dead in the water.

Johnson pushed himself away from the table and stood up. He removed the cuffs around Anakova’s wrists and opened the door. Clauson and Anakova looked at each other, and slowly rose out of their chairs before adjusting their coats and clothing.

As they made their way into the hall, Tim Johnson said, “The prosecutor will probably be calling you to explain any charges.”

Anakova stopped and turned to face Johnson who was leaning against the doorjamb. Dimitri Anakova put his fingers into the shape of a gun and pointed at Johnson, pulling an imaginary trigger as he smiled.

Johnson never changed his expression as the two men walked past the remaining officer at the front desk and out the front door.

Anakova and Clauson made their way out to the parking lot—Anakova to his Escalade and Clauson to his Range Rover. They pulled out of the lot onto Lake Street and then drove south on US-31. Before driving through Boyne Falls on US-131, they turned left onto Thumb Lake Road with the Range Rover in the lead. Another quick right and they were in the cemetery. John Brooks followed slowly, but remained eastbound on Thumb Lake Road. The Escalade was still clearly marked on his phone.

Anakova pulled ahead, parked in front of Clauson’s vehicle, stepped out, and got into the Range Rover. He knew his SUV was compromised. There was another man in the backseat who Anakova did not know.

Anakova got in the front with Clauson. No lights. No reflections. Just slight clicks as doors quietly opened and shut.

The flashes from the .22 were barely visible outside the Range Rover's blackened windows. There was no sound audible from outside either. The Rover started up and slowly turned west and then south on US-131. There seemed to be no hurry.

Brooks waited momentarily. No movement from the Escalade. There was only one return on the Range Rover's Illinois plates: owned by Robert James Clauson, Attorney, Chicago. Still seeing no movement from the Escalade, Brooks got out of his Buick and made his way through a neighboring cornfield toward the cemetery. He climbed a fence a distance away from the vehicle's line of sight and pulled his weapon. Gloves on, he slowly walked toward the truck and quickly yanked the door open. He was already convinced his man was gone.

The empty SUV proved his premonition correct. No sign of anyone. Dimitri Anakova's phone was on the passenger seat, and keys were in the ignition. Brooks checked the phone. The SIM card was gone. Everything else was clean. No coffee cups, no candy wrappers, no cigarette butts in the ashtray.

After looking around the perimeter without disturbing footprints or tire tracks in the sandy gravel, Brooks holstered his weapon. Returning to the open driver's door of the Escalade, he leaned against it with his right leg crossed over his left ankle and his right arm resting on top of the window.

"Well, now," he said to himself. He knew the Range Rover was long gone.

After a long, hot bath; a foot rub; and full body massage, Sam was relaxed and lying on Parker's chest. Breaths were slow and even from both.

"Are you still going to attend the hearing tomorrow in Lansing?" Parker asked.

"Yes. I have to be there. Between almost getting blown up and then stalked, it'll feel like a vacation." Sam's eyes were closed.

"All of your friends driving together?"

"Yes. And I'm just a passenger."

"Good."
"You know if I don't go they win?"
"I know."
"You'd go?"
"Yeah."
"That's why I'm going."
After a few minutes, they were both asleep.

# FIFTEEN

**PRIVATE** WAS POSTED ON A SIGN OUTSIDE THE WINDOWless meeting room at Genève Aéroport in Switzerland. It was late and both men had flown in for an emergency meeting where no one else would have contact or knowledge. Sir Edward and Evgeny sat across from each other at a small, brown, square office table. Sir Edward was rubbing his palms together with his elbows on the table. He was waiting for Evgeny to retrieve some final details from his phone.

"Evgeny," he whispered, "we're on limited time here."

Evgeny gestured one moment with his right index finger.

Sir Edward stopped rubbing his palms and began to massage his cheeks. His eyes were closed as his agitation grew.

"Evgeny!" he whispered louder.

No response.

Evgeny turned his body sideways, away from the distractions of his colleague.

Sir Edward couldn't get the phone conversation with John Stanley out of his thoughts. It was a risk, but a well-measured risk–so he thought. Stanley had a penchant for oil and gas, and word in the billionaire community was that he was looking for a resting place, a sentimental way to spend his remaining years in retirement. Sir Edward wasn't aware of John Stanley's life change. Only John Stanley knew about his inoperable cancer. Stanley had watched the communities in Northern Michigan and other locales around the country dry up from no employment, and billionaire John Stanley had led the charge for bigger profits, bigger business, and greater investments–all overseas with cheaper labor—for years. But with mortality staring him down, he now felt responsible. Only so much charity work and donations to local food pantries made up for the true cause of the problem.

Sir Edward's conscience was now full of his very loud thoughts telling him that the Stanley call was a mistake. Finally, he reached across the table and in one fluid motion, grabbed Evgeny's phone and threw it against the wall. Stunned, Evgeny turned wide-eyed at the super PAC leader.

"Goddamn it, Evgeny!" Sir Edward straightened his tie and made sure his suit coat was proportionally hanging on both sides of his chair. "It's my time now," he said softly in a calm, methodical voice.

The ex-KGB and current Russian billionaire stared at his friend. He waited for Sir Edward to talk.

"I'm quite sorry, Evgeny, but I am limited on time and wish to express a concern. I also want to hear about your man in Michigan. But first, I made a call to a colleague in the States about joining our group. It was against our group's agreement since he is an American, but I felt it necessary since most of our fracking operations are there. Anyway, I believe something may be wrong."

"And?"

"Nothing. Just want to make sure I've communicated this in person and not via phone."

"Do we need to watch Mr. Stanley?"

"I don't know. I would like a little more consultation. Where are we in Michigan?"

"Not good, but not to worry."

"Meaning?" Sir Edward sat back in his chair awaiting the worst.

Evgeny moved forward, placed his forearms on the table, and clasped his hands. "Temporarily out of service. We've had to … we've had to make some adjustments. It was fortuitous; however, legal was in the area and we sent a second man with him. The message is being delivered as we speak."

"Message?"

"Someone was intruding too far."

"It is becoming tenuous in some states, Evgeny. We've stayed out of the federal government, but we must be careful as we sow the ground at the state level. We cannot afford any mistakes." Sir Edward was now sitting up, almost nose to nose with Evgeny.

"We are protected, and everyone under Grand Rapids Resources. No links. Our operatives know that—they understand their role."

Sir Edward placed both palms on the top of the table in proportional distances. He glanced at both hands to double check their geography on the table. “Once before, I assumed all was well.” He looked up at Evgeny. Their faces were square to each other and eyes ratcheted. “Once before, I was assured all was well before being snatched up in an elevator, carted off for pictures in a brothel, and being dumped in an alley. The next thing I know, Rupert Murdoch has photos of me plastered from London to Hong Kong and from New York to Honolulu.”

“I assure you, Sir Edward, I— we—are in control of the situation. After the hearing in Michigan, we shut everything off and new encryptions begin. If the NSA is around, they won’t be.” Evgeny never blinked.

“Right. Well, we are winning legislatively in each state; but public opinion can change quickly. However, if our path is followed, the old U. S. of A. will soon be producing more energy than the Middle East or Russia, and of course our little group will continue to use those profits for political placements.” Sir Edward sat back and grinned. “Oh, Evgeny, this IS too easy.”

“We have assistance and will be perfect. Please. I am sure of it.”

Sir Edward nodded, tipped back in his chair, and reached behind for the phone. “Two Stoli. Neat.” Sir Edward tipped back toward the table. “Spaseeba.”

“Pazhalsta.” Evgeny laughed. “Pazhalsta.”

*The drill begins quickly and moves steadily through the sand and into the water table. Mud, sand; dirt. Rock. Thin, thick, porous, hard, then solid. More solid. Hollows quietly pop. Heat. More soft pops and hollows. The drill slowly drives. One thousand. Two thousand. Six thousand feet. It twists and the engineers turn the bit. Horizontal, another mile or so. Dense and black. Rock millions and billions of years old, shattered and pulverized. The irony of the silence: To create the constant noise above, the place of energy is no matter. It's what makes money. Dorian Gray's land on the Manistee River is the new place. In fact, there is a pipe …*

# SIXTEEN

**FRIDAY, APRIL 15**

"THIS MEETING IS CALLED TO ORDER. MAY WE HAVE THE roll?"

"Representative Williams?"

"Here."

"Representative Carmichael?"

"Present."

The roll call ended.

"We welcome all to this meeting of the Public Energy Commission for the State of Michigan," said Bruce Harvey, House Majority Whip and soon-to-be termed-out representative from Grand Rapids. "We are a joint committee made up of both House and Senate members chosen by their respective parties. Our mission during this legislative session is to mediate a series of bills given to both sides of the state legislature to control and/or regulate hydraulic fracturing for natural gas and oil."

Everyone in the room listened to the pro forma speech. The heart of the matter was why the room was so packed that several people had to stand outside in the hallway.

"This Committee is hopefully a short-term group." Harvey surveyed the crowd. "Perhaps we'll start with some opening remarks, then move directly into motions. Might I remind you, this meeting is not for public comment."

Bruce Harvey wasn't worried about the way the day would proceed, or end. The discussion with fellow members prior to the session provided a well-rehearsed plan to make sure the results of the hearing would materialize precisely as manipulated. All but the most trivial hearings were planned this way. The public was pretty much fodder for the members, staff, and lobby core who provided the reality.

This early spring day in Lansing was unusually warm and sunny.

People wanted to be outside. Sessions were shortened to allow for lots of free time for the legislators; however, the governor had his majority party on a short leash these days since coming from the private business community, he wished to have all of his functions more closely resemble a for-profit business model rather than a lumbering bureaucracy. It had become a typical roller-coaster ride for Michigan. The Dems in, things slowed down. The GOP in, things sped up. The problem was that each new administration changed everything, so most of the communities, staff, and bureaucrats sat back and became frustrated. Making the problem worse? Term limits. The loam for lobbyists in Michigan was fertile. The arena for outside influence was wide open.

"With the permission of his colleagues, Senator Van Der Knacht has been holding public hearings around the state. He would like to comment first on these meetings ... I hear no objection ..." After a brief pause, "Please proceed."

Sam Moore and her three friends sat in the middle rows of the hearing room. They arrived an hour early to make sure they could sit on the wooden benches versus leaning against a wall or hanging outside the door in the hallway.

"Thank you, Mr. Chairman. Yes, I've been humbled by the allowance to travel this great State of Michigan." The TV cameras and radio microphones were front and center, so the egos were running high. "I've traveled from Lake Superior to Lake Erie and from Lake Michigan over to Lake Huron."

Sam wanted to jump up out of her chair. Instead she leaned over to her friend Delores on her left. "Is this guy serious?" Sam whispered. "Hand-picked audiences. Hand-picked questions. Cutting time for any dissenters." She looked up and smiled at the oratory. "Asshole," she said through her teeth.

Delores kept her stare straight ahead. As Sam finished her diatribe, Delores poked her in the ribs with her elbow.

After ticking off the entire list of places he had visited, Dutch Van Der Knacht continued. "The last forum held in Frederic is probably the best example to use for a general description as to how the public feels. We had a standing-room-only crowd with only one person speaking against the use of hydraulic fracturing." The good Senator from Grand Rapids turned his gaze directly at Sam. To make the moment more dramatic, he paused. All the politicos, lobbyists, representatives, and others on the bench noticed.

In her steely confidence and mastered assertiveness, Sam didn't twitch. As if wearing an impenetrable shield of righteousness, she remained calm, but her three friends squirmed at the attention.

Standing in four different places around the room were the lobbyists under contract from GRR and hired with money laundered from Resources For All. The lobbyists didn't need to look at Sam. They knew who she was, where she was, and what she was going to do next. Thus the four men dressed in dark Armani suits continued to look at Dutch Van Der Knacht and the other bought members to make sure they followed through with their secured motions and votes at this hearing.

After briefly referring to his notes, the senator continued. "Our citizens across this state have a need *and* a desire to *work*, *make money*, and be a *productive part* of this growing economy. For instance, in the Township of Frederic, seventy-five people packed a small township hall and applauded at a chance to be gainfully employed. They have at least five businesses boarded-up in their small downtown, and an unemployment, or underemployment, rate close to fifty percent. A new arena of natural gas exploration would restore this fine, patriotic, upstanding community to its fullest potential."

There were several knocks on the centuries-old dark tables where the members were seated; and some random applause from around the room. The lobby core stood against their respective walls with their arms folded.

"Thank you, Senator Van Der Knacht. Any other comments to his introductory foray?"

"I believe," said Glen Howard, the Representative from Crawford County, where Frederic resides as its poorest township, "that our colleague from Grand Rapids speaks for all of us. We've all heard the same positive responses." He looked up and down the tables at his fellow lawmakers. "There has been a smattering of dissenting opinions expressed to all of us by a connected lot of environmental lobby groups, constituents, and other misinformed public." He was taking as many pot shots as possible since there would be no retort from the public at this meeting, and all of the standing committee rules were re-written as soon as the new gubernatorial administration had taken office three years prior. He continued, "We believe Senator Van Der Knacht has found a solution to the reason for this Conference Committee. He has heroically preceded us and placed his face in full public view to absorb the slings and arrows of this now noncontroversial, fact-driven science so that we may lift the economy of this state to its once proud standing as a leader in the United States of America."

Louder knocks on the tables and more applause from the crowd, with most people standing and applauding. Sam and her crew stayed seated. One could feel the heat rising from the top of Sam's head, but never a chance of anyone seeing her emotions. Not a smile. Not a frown. No expression at all.

*Parker was right,* she thought. *This was all staged for the cameras and audience and directed by the boys in suits in the far corners of the room. The same thing he used to do.*

"The Chair applauds the comments of our Representative from Crawford County. As I look around the room, I believe we are in agreement thus far. If there are no objections, we'll proceed to public testimony at a time to be determined after one more visit to Frederic by our esteemed colleague from Grand Rapids." With that said, his gavel poised the entire time, it found the pedestal and ended the meeting.

It was over in the blink of an eye with language and direction spoken so rapidly in between and after such longwinded comments, that a person who didn't grasp the system would be totally clueless. It was as well-scripted an affair as had ever been rehearsed in the back rooms to which the public had no admission. As the conference room cleared, Sam sat. Her friends stood and watched others chit-chat in small groups, shake hands, and make plans for evening martinis at Troppo on Michigan Avenue. Most of the lobbyists in the room were tanned from wintering or vacationing somewhere warm, most likely with legislators in tow. Reporters were busy with microphones, phones, and notepads taking comments from legislators whose staff members were pushing and shoving to get their boss interviewed first.

Sam stood and realized her battle must be taken to a different front. A different reality. The governor and GRR had the skids greased. All the public testimony in the world wasn't going to change the vote. Parker was right. Follow the money trail backward and find a good investigative reporter to blow the whistle. She looked around and thought, *Don't trust anyone in this room. I wish Parker was here, but he can't be, and I need to do this.*

Sam exited the room with her friends to join the martini groups at Troppo.

Sir Edward sat on his private jet in southeastern Turkmenistan. The country, made up of five provinces, housed its capital in Ashgabat, which was over two hundred miles east of the smaller gas fields in southeastern Turkmenistan. Since its revival and independence in 1991, Turkmenistan had become one of the top five natural gas producers in the world. Not only was Sir Edward's company one of the main producers of energy there, his company was now helping China, Russia, the U.S., and others export this energy, unaware that a good portion of those profits made their way into the Resources For All super PAC to influence the politics in each of those countries.

His plane had become more of a home. He lived on it for weeks at a time if necessary, and there was comfort knowing he could leave and be anywhere whenever he wished.

At 3:30 a.m., it was black outside except for the lights from the wells and drilling teams working twenty-four hours seven days a week. Sir Edward hated coming to the fields. They were dirty, smelly, and full of workers who gazed at him through the blackened windows of the SUVs that were transported for his benefit wherever he traveled. He came to appease Nazar, a new member of Resources For All, whose desire to live in the outback city of Serhetabat placed him in direct vision of the new pipeline that supplied India, Pakistan, and Afghanistan. His pipeline. The one Sir Edward wanted.

Three hours until sunrise, but Sir Edward couldn't sleep. He sipped his Hendricks and thought about the trip through the fields. His entourage of white SUVs would wind its way around wellheads, drilling platforms, and the emotionless eyes of the men who worked long hours. His bodyguards wore navy blue suits and were ex-special forces from wherever he could hire them. They were paid six-figure salaries and were taken care of like gladiators.

His Bombardier XRS jet made the trips to smaller airports while his Boeing Business jet, a personalized 747, made trips where he needed to haul vehicles. The runway at Serhetabat could handle his 747, so there he sat. He experienced no emotion as he watched the blackened faces of the men staring at him while he sat in comfort. A comfort he deserved. After all, they wouldn't have jobs without his company. They wouldn't be able to light their lamps or cook their food.

The sunrise would bring his bodyguards to the stairs of the jet. They would stand like soldiers, facing outward to protect his life. He would climb into his white Suburban and his driver would take him to Nazar's palace.

The men that worked at wellhead 27 were always watchful. They would stop working and stand up straight to stare. It was clear they were angry, but why? After the entourage would pass, Sir Edward would look behind and see the men work with renewed energy. They would be chanting something he couldn't understand. Then he would notice other work crews they passed chanting and working just as hard. He'd smile and believe his presence was a positive reinforcement, a motivation to them.

He'd think of the meeting. A bore. Why not on some island or in Dubai? Nazar was always suspicious of the other group members. He wouldn't say it at the meetings, so he would gossip and share his conspiracies with Sir Edward alone—but Nazar continued to send millions to the super PAC. He knew the West was the enemy, and the only way to defeat the West was within their own political machines. Sir Edward agreed, but Sir Edward's motive was profit–no matter the source.

The Framingham family was of aristocracy and dated its land holdings as rewards for assisting Henry VIII. Sir Edward had never worked a physical job in his life. His toughest test was long hours of study toward his doctorate in economics from Oxford and a stint with MI6. As a six-foot-two, straight, and rigid frame of long British descent, he made for an imposing figure to most. His sports included rugby and soccer, but his claim to fame was in the scull. His one-man boat was never defeated and, just like his business ideals and created political power, they would never be defeated as long as he was around. The NSA got close, but money was power and he had more than anyone–including most countries.

He would spend time with Nazar, drink his vodka, and return watching the men work. As the jet would take off, he would be in the comfort of his monitors, phone, and Hendricks. The smelly and hellish community would be out of sight and out of mind. No towns. No hedgerows or small, romantic villages. Only detestable communities of boards, aluminum, and outdoor latrines. Detestable.

Sir Edward sat back in his leather swivel chair. He pulled the shade on the window to darken his in-flight study. *Detestable.*

"Sir, you'd better come down here. There's been a change."

John Mansfield was putting on his jacket when the speaker on his phone sounded. He reached down and picked up the receiver to speak with Evans. "And?"

"The John Brooks' assignment and our connections through London, Moscow, Dubai, and Michigan—they're dead. Gone."

"I'll be right there." Mansfield hung his jacket back up and walked calmly out of the room, pushed the elevator button, and spoke into his cell phone, "Honey, I won't be home for dinner."

ſ ſ ſ

John Brooks didn't need to be told there was a change in his assignment. The man he had been following had disappeared into thin air. The Range Rover was found halfway between Grand Rapids and Frederic. No prints. No bodies. Nothing. The attorney the vehicle was registered to was also missing. Brooks checked himself into the Amway Grand in downtown Grand Rapids and made a phone call.

"Director Johnson? This is John Brooks again. I believe you've worked extensively with my partner, Todd Ramsey? I have a favor to ask concerning Sam Moore."

ſ ſ ſ

Parker packed a suitcase, confirmed his flight plans, and printed his ticket for Washington. Once he knew Sam was okay in Lansing, he would leave from the Pellston Airport, arrive at Reagan International in D.C., and stay the night with his son in Foggy Bottom.

"Sam?"

"Hi, honey. I'm fine. The girls and I are finishing a martini dinner."

Parker could hear giggles in the background. "Okay. You be safe. We'll talk later about how it went." Parker was putting on his coat and reaching for his suitcase with the phone cradled between his shoulder and his ear.

"No. We don't have to. Nothing happened. Just like you said. You enjoy your son. Love you."

The call ended and Parker looked outside at the sunset. He put the phone in his pocket, made sure the cats were inside and had food, then he walked out the back door. He left for the airport feeling confident someone or something was going to keep Sam safe the couple days he would be gone.

*They sit in their offices, a world apart from the gas and oilfields in lands they've never seen. Constituent calls and visits are handled by staff; people placated while other staff members take calls from the monied few who have given to the campaign—untraceable. Stock portfolios grow and incomes are shared for continued political power. It becomes less and less about the people of the land and more about profits. A détente is reached in state legislatures; no one tells on the other about using staff for fundraising or "development" of funders. CNN, MSNBC, and FOX all become the ESPN of the politicos—less and less about the voters. Fame and fortune were always one election away for any of the players in the game.*

# SEVENTEEN

**SATURDAY, APRIL 16**

PARKER SPENT THE NIGHT AT HIS SON'S CONDO AT THE Avenue on I Street in Foggy Bottom. He took his dollar down the stairs for an organic coffee at Whole Foods.

The sky was gray after a morning rain, puddles were plenty, and rainwater was still running in the streets along the curbs. Parker's Merrells and dark-green Mountain Hardwear raincoat evoked a purposeful appearance as a man from a place far north of the Mason-Dixon Line. Most other patrons were dressed in black: black-wool pea coats or black fleeces with black or blue jeans and black shoes or boots. The black North Face all-season jacket was popular at this time of year. He looked at a woman walking into Whole Foods wearing a long, yellow wool coat. She looked like a newly hatched chicken floating in a sea of black, and a smile came to Parker as he wondered if the coat was to loathe forty-degree weather yet still celebrate a spring day. The black was boring, but the yellow was really out of place.

As Parker silently touted his northerly appearance, he stood in line at Whole Foods awaiting the Orwellian call to the cash register. It was all he could do to stand there in his misanthropic aura, and smile while awaiting the robotic tone emanating from the speakers. But it did alleviate the pressure of the job at hand.

Parker made his way to 15th Street and the Treasury Building, where he had a quiet moment several years ago as he made his way into his recovery. A quilted North Face with red trim highlighting the black walked toward him on 15th. Both ears of the young man held white ear buds from an iPhone he carried. Parker walked past the spot where, five years ago, he decided to change his life forever—the very spot next to Alexander Hamilton's gift to the United States, the very spot where

Parker Moore decided to set a new goal: give up all he had and work toward zero. Back to his kids. Back to the rhythms of a life he'd forgotten. He stopped and looked at the corner of the stone-faced side; the deep recesses of the ridge he had grabbed that day in emotional pain. His life from that moment changed as he predicted; now, out of his purgatory, he smiled and relished the decision.

Black trench coats and black umbrellas filled the sidewalks and street at 1:00 p.m. as he walked south toward Constitution Avenue. His appointment at the Capital Club was at 3:00 p.m. He realized there could be a dress code, but the check he carried in his pocket didn't care about gabardine or denim, and the senator he was meeting would make allowances.

To be back in D.C., after his last public appearance at the Senate Select Committee on Intelligence, had Parker thinking about all of the changes in his life since then. House members had resigned. Senators had given up re-election campaigns, and one Supreme Court Justice committed suicide after his arrest by the FBI. The cold-hearted Jack Fletcher said it was the saddest day of his life as a special agent.

Parker walked past the Smithsonian, remembering his meeting with John Brooks after the NSA cut him loose. Four years later, he sat next to Brooks at the Senate hearing blowing the lid off super PACs. He hadn't seen Todd Ramsey since that day; but Brooks had been a frequent visitor up north for fishing and relaxation. The occasional email and phone call rounded out a nice, comfortable friendship. Now, one agent was everywhere Parker went, and the other nowhere to be seen, which could be a good thing.

Parker proceeded past the south side of the Capitol Building and the Metro stop. He could have easily taken the Metro, but the catharsis needed to happen on his walk. As a true romantic, he wouldn't pass up a chance to relive significant tangible memories for a train ride.

By the time he reached the Capital Club, the sky had decided to drown Washington D.C. His raincoat held out the moisture, but his jeans were soaked. A flash of lightning and a crack of thunder sounded as he walked under the canopy and touched the front door. It was as if Damian was entering a church.

"Can I help you, sir?" asked the concierge in a well-pressed suit, his eyes looking at Parker with disdain.

"Yes, thank you. I'm here to see Senator William Coolridge. He's expecting me."

The concierge continued staring at Parker without moving. His well-pressed suit still well-pressed.

"Sir, I assure you the good Senator is waiting. If you please." Parker was now towering over the young man dripping water all over his desk.

He quickly wiped off the water. "I'll check."

Parker waited as the man pressed a few buttons on the phone and turned as he talked softly into the receiver. He turned back to face Parker.

"He's waiting for you. Second floor, room three. He said the scotch will be familiar."

"Thanks." Parker took his coat off and shook it over the concierge's desk. "Oh, I'm sorry. Can't take me anywhere." Parker smiled at the well-pressed suit that now dripped with water.

The concierge never moved.

Parker made his way up the stairs while trying to straighten his hair.

"Parker! Moore, you sonovabitch. I'm surprised they let you in here."

"Senator."

"Here. Sit here. The Lagavulin's poured."

"Thanks, Bill. Feels good to be back."

"Nobody took a shot at you, I hope," Senator Coolridge said as the two sat in the Queen Anne leather chairs by the fireplace. "I'm figuring the Capitol shook as you walked by," the Senator said laughing loudly.

"Only a few pieces of marble fell, but your concierge is calling out a contract I'm sure," Parker responded, smiling. He then closed his eyes momentarily, turning his head to the fire, and put himself in the moment.

"Moore, you don't change. How are you doing, really? You've been to hell and back while the rest of us just keep watching."

"I'm very well. Best actually," Parker said as he looked into the senator's eyes. "It's time to get back into the fray."

"You have the check?"

"I do."

Senator William Coolridge, from the great state of Wyoming, was the Chair of the Senate Commerce Committee and also happened to be the Chair of the Republican National Committee. At six foot four, he was nearly the same size as Parker Moore. His stature hadn't lost an inch, even at seventy years old, and his voice still boomed as a base speaker in the back of a low-rider. A rancher by trade, he used his voice at long ranges for everything from cattle to Democrats.

"Okay, Parker. Now what's Stanley want?"

*Water. It's all about the water. If there is fracking, there is a need for water; and Michigan has more water than anyone. Proximity to wells wouldn't matter, and there wouldn't be any outcry about the Ogallala Aquifers. Michigan needed money. Detroit was in shambles. Drilling and pipes meant jobs. If the water could be taken slowly and blamed on climate change, who would care as long as the money flowed? It always came down to water. There was lots of water in Michigan.*

# EIGHTEEN

**TUESDAY, APRIL 19**

AFTER HIS RETURN FROM WASHINGTON D. C., NO THREATS to Sam or him, and no sign of John Brooks, Parker found himself in Petoskey sitting on a bench at the end of the pier. It was one of his favorite spots to sit with binoculars and watch the birds come and go while the journal was always at hand for poems popping into the frontal cortex.

*The wind was tempestuous this clear day ...*

He wrote as he looked around the harbor. The wind flipped pages as he tried to write.

*Cirrus clouds floated high above ...*

He watched people walk the breakwater. Behind him the clock-tower at the entrance to the pier struck 2:00 p.m. Some fishermen cast twelve-foot poles toward the water, hoping lure and line would entice steelhead or anything else that would create a fight. Grebes in transit to nesting grounds dove through the ripples on Lake Michigan looking for lunch, and a Goldeneye duck landed to Parker's right. Binoculars up. It would be one already recorded in his bird count for the spring. As the duck preened, Parker gazed past it at the water. What would become of these lakes? Ten thousand years young after the last Ice Age. What would oil and gas exploration create or damage? The water clarity allowed him to watch the ducks dive, swim, and search for food without the aid of polarized sunglasses. For a couple of centuries now boats, cities, and factories have dumped myriad substances. Some invisible yet harmful–mercury, insecticides, you name it.

Fracking was another story. Unlisted chemicals soured the ground and all the waters connected. Estuaries and feeder streams unable to taste the poison they carried. Up until now, a watchful public had stopped Lake Erie from catching on fire and enjoyed their shimmering jewels of fresh water. Now, the enemy was inland. The companies had a new tactic of drawing down water and pumping in chemicals for gas and oil regurgitation. What was worse is the connection to jobs and income for people who had neither—trading the soul for liquid poison that paid for a new car or a large-screen TV.

He thought of Sam fighting the public's fight while he choked on his spit and went back into the game to watch her back. The silent war, unknown to the public until some cub reporter wanted to make a splash. Then it was all about the splash and not the facts of the subject. America was always behind on the details. Now Parker was setting up a super PAC to fight with another super PAC while the original Super PAC sat in Fort Meade, Maryland, picking sides. He felt a connection through all of the chaos to protect his home. Not just his and Sam's, but the lakes. Parker's family had been around these Great Lakes for over one hundred and fifty years. *They* were his home.

ϯ ϯ ϯ

"Quiet, John. Not a thing happening." Tim Johnson was driving home after attending a Chief's Association meeting in Lansing.

"Same here." John Brooks had seen all of Grand Rapids that he wanted to and was ready to head north. "Is Parker back?"

"Yes."

"K. I'll be in Grayling by tonight. We'll touch base tomorrow." Brooks looked out over the namesake Grand River from his hotel window high above the city.

"Fine. Keep an eye on the house?"

"Please. Something isn't right."

"Let's hope it stays quiet. Maybe it's over. Later."

The call ended, but the thought of a trillion-dollar super PAC and its connected money sources going quiet was not reality and John Brooks knew it.

ϯ ϯ ϯ

After a long, relaxing dinner, Sam was in much better spirits about her trip to Lansing. Parker was reading Robert Service, and she was next to him in bed reading the newspaper while commenting on the letters to the editor, something about the stupid lighthouse in the park. Parker couldn't get Pat Coruthers and Sir Edward Framingham out of his mind; Coruthers' voice and his face wouldn't leave his thoughts. He tried getting deeper into the "Cremation of Sam Magee," but it was difficult when the poem was in rote memory. The attorney that was supposed to visit Kathi hadn't called her back; all was too quiet. Parker was determined to make sure he used the time wisely.

"There's a guy," Parker said as he continued looking at his book. His upper body had slouched down on the three pillows between his head and the headboard of the bed.

"A guy?" Sam didn't take her eyes off the paper, and even turned the page.

"Yeah. You know. A guy."

"Parker," she said as she took off her glasses and turned toward him, "this sounds like an old mafia movie."

"His name is Bobby. About five four, white hair, perpetual tan, always smoking a little Hemingway cigar, although he likes any kind anyone sends him. Collects the bands like trophies."

"So?" The *Petoskey News & Review* was set aside.

"We may need him."

"We? For what?"

"Kathi's store."

"Why? She doesn't sell cigars."

"That was a clue to his largess of money. You didn't see as many gangster films as I did."

"Okay." Paper was back up.

"If Coruthers is the skunk I think he is, we need to find an investor for her store. Bobby's the guy. Just a matter of interest rates."

"Are you going to tell her?" Paper back down.

"When the time's right." Parker never put down Robert Service.

"It's what you do best, Parker. Making sure everybody is taken care of." Paper back up.

"Yeah. 'Cept me." He put the book down and stared at Keeper lying at his feet.

*Developing natural gas from shale involves eight distinct steps. First, the leases are signed by the landowners and permits are drawn from regulatory agencies. Next, the well pad is constructed; multiple wells can be drilled from a single pad. The third part is the actual drilling, which is down then horizontal up to a mile each way. The fourth step provides for the hydraulic fracturing or "fracking" while pipelines are constructed to supply gas to market. After the gas begins to flow, the fracking fluid (millions and millions of gallons of water and chemical slurry) needs to be stored or treated. In the meantime, state legislators write and pass legislation bypassing EPA standards and other regulatory measures to protect the fracking process and disregard the groundwater used for drinking and other public purposes. The legislators, with campaign financing provided by gas-producing companies, believe the companies to be honest and truthful with their insistence on the safety of the practice; therefore, little regulation should be necessary. The sixth step leaves a working well, but the surrounding landscape is reclaimed for the public's use and for aesthetic value. The seventh step to the fracking process is the varied time of a productive well–it could be years. Finally, the eighth step is capping and the reclamation of a well site after production has ceased. If all events occur as scheduled and without error, the fracking is considered successful; however, not all companies follow the rules, and the water is forever gone from human use …*

# NINETEEN

WEDNESDAY, APRIL 20

"BOBBY?" PARKER WAS ON LAKE STREET OUTSIDE KATHI'S store.

"Moore." Bobby was at Cava in Bay Harbor, sitting outside with his phone on speaker.

"Got a minute?"

"For you, always." Bobby reached down and took his phone off speaker.

"If someone I know needs some emergency financing for a store because something bad may happen to her investor …"

"How much?" Bobby Alex cut Parker's question short. He sat back in his seat outside Cava's side patio with his sunglasses on, and his reading glasses on his head. The Hemingway cigar was twirled between his right thumb and finger as he puffed long and slow. Bobby Alex didn't fake it—he inhaled every puff.

"Not sure. Can I ask it not matter?" Parker leaned against the wall, staring at the empty hole in the ground known as the Petoskey Pit that was supposed to be a condo and shopping center before the money went dry. Now it was nothing but a block-wide hole with a green fence around it.

"Sure. Friend of yours?" Bobby put the cigar down for a moment and adjusted the collar of his North Face fleece. Sitting outside in April didn't matter. The shorts were on for a warm day, but the wind would bring a chill off the water.

"Sam's."

"She's covered."

"I owe ya, Bobby."

"Moore, you're always good for it. We'll talk." Bobby had the cigar back in his mouth.

"Hey, Bobby?" Parker could hear the long draw on the cigar. "You know those things'll kill ya."

"The least of my worries. Good afternoon, Mr. Moore."

Parker turned and looked into the shop window adorned with a china cabinet, sofa, various pillows, linens, dishes, and glasses. It looked like a Norman Rockwell painting. He took a deep breath and walked into the store. Kathi was showing off some lavender soap paraphernalia to some Victorian-era ladies who looked like they may have actually known Old Vicky.

"Excuse me." Parker smiled at the two women. "Kathi, can I borrow you for a minute?"

"How's the store these days, Kathi?" Parker's head was on a swivel looking at the hundreds of items finely positioned for prime aesthetic value as they walked toward the back of the store.

"It's so good! I just wish I knew why this lawyer guy was coming to visit." Kathi stood with her hands on her hips. She peeked out toward the front to make sure the ladies couldn't hear her, even though she knew they wouldn't have heard an atomic bomb outside the front door. "Sorry. I wanna be careful."

"Would you trust me, Kathi, if I told you no matter what happens, your store will be okay and remain in your hands?" Parker picked up an *Architectural Digest* and looked at the front cover.

"Oh, Parker. Is it going to be that bad?" Kathi yelled as she slumped onto a loveseat in the back of the store.

"Shhhh." Parker looked up and noticed the ladies picking up some lavender soaps.

"Oh, shit. They can't hear themselves think. Now, what's going on?"

"Honestly? I have no idea, but I want you to feel secure. I've made some arrangements; so feel secure."

"Okay." Kathi wiped away some tears. "Okay." She took a deep breath and kissed Parker on the cheek while she hugged him. Parker was bending down as far as he could to reach Kathi's small stature.

"You take care." Parker walked to the front and opened the door to step outside.

"Thanks, Parker," Kathi yelled as she walked toward the women. "Now, what have you decided on?"

The two women giggled and looked at each other. Then they both turned toward Kathi and pointed behind their shoulders at the door.

"Him," they said in unison.

ſ ſ ſ

It was about 10:00 p.m. when he walked into Cava with his lady of the night. He looked no one in the eye. She was six feet in flats to his six foot four. Her chest was a double D to his fifty-six inches. Both would fill up a dining chair, and it wasn't all adipose tissue.

Parker Moore, helping out as maître d' for the night, greeted the couple at the door.

"Good evening. Dinner? Drinks?"

"That table. There." The man pointed at a window table with his thick finger.

The woman looked at Parker, smiled, and rolled her eyes.

"Very well. That table is yours." Parker led them to the requested spot, knowing it was already reserved. He'd make adjustments. As he set down two menus, he called to the head server, "Melissa. Two, thank you. Champagne, please." He winked as he walked by her.

The man sat down and shoved extra plates and glasses aside before Melissa could remove them from the four-top. Parker came back with a wine list, and the man looked up and made eye contact. Parker glared right back at him. The man looked like he'd bit the curb more than once in his life.

"Frank and I will need a moment," said the woman, smiling and trying to break the chill.

Parker bowed in a respectful manner, then walked toward the concierge desk where he saw a black stretch limo pulling up to the front entrance. His phone vibrated in his pocket, but he didn't check it. He knew what to do.

He walked back over to the table. "Sir, if I may. There's a call for the lady." The couple looked at each other. The man seemed to understand.

"Thank you. I know where the phone is." The woman looked across the table and gave the man a flirtatious smile dripping with sex. "I'll be right back."

As soon as the woman came out to the bar and asked for the phone, Melissa escorted her around the back behind a curtain. Parker remained at the table as the man stared at the menu. The discomfort was thick.

With the gentleman facing the back of the restaurant, he didn't see Bobby walk in with two tall military types in navy blue suits at his side. When Parker pulled out the lady's chair; the man looked relieved thinking his date had returned, but as soon as he saw Bobby out of the corner of his eye he looked surprised. The man started to stand up and Parker placed his hand on the man's right shoulder and firmly held him down. Suddenly the man was surrounded by three men over six foot five and seven hundred and fifty pounds of flesh.

Bobby sat down softly and quietly. Patrons in the dining room seemed unaware—or ignored the ordeal knowing Bobby was involved.

"Frank," Bobby said as he brought out a cigar.

"Bobby," answered Frank.

In the next moment, the two suits had Frank away from the table and out the back door. The few people at the bar in the front of the restaurant never knew what happened. At Frank's exit, the woman returned with Melissa. Parker pulled Frank's chair out and gestured for the woman to sit.

"Thank you, Bobby," she said.

"Amanda. How are you?"

Although her date had changed, she wasn't upset. She didn't like Frank, and no one would see Frank again.

As Parker turned to walk away, Bobby grabbed his arm. "We're even, Mr. Moore." Bobby turned to continue his conversation with his date.

Parker smiled, straightened his tie à la James Bond, and walked over to Jette at the bar and asked for a martini. "Shaken. Not stirred."

"Parker, shut up." Jette turned and grabbed the Bombay gin.

Late at night, in the bowels of NSA, the staff was staring at monitors, big screens on the walls, and white boards with marker streaks connecting numerous places around the globe. Nothing. Supervisor Evans rubbed her chin. All was silent from GRR and Resources For All. So quiet, it was unsettling.

*The leases and regulatory requirements did not always fall in order, nor did construction. With so many wells and sites, inspectors lost track of who was where and who was supposed to be where. Plus a lease might cover a well pad but not the land a mile away underground. In the name of profit, all was fair in love and war.*

# TWENTY

THURSDAY, APRIL 21

PARKER WAS SCOUTING TRANSPORTATION IDEAS, LAND access, and building sites for John Stanley's project. Sam was along for the ride.

"Hey, let's have a beer before we head back," Parker said as he turned into the Swamp's parking lot.

It was a chilly night, and the bar was full of locals. For most, the Swamp was their second home. The bar stools were occupied as well as the tables near the pool table. Sam and Parker found a vacant two-top in the front corner. Behind them was a large, round table full of militia members.

"Gray is just gone, I'm tellin' ya," a camo-clothed woman said loud enough for Parker to hear.

Parker did not turn around but he listened.

"Why do you think he's gone?" asked another woman as she tabled her PBR.

"Cause his fucking house is blown up! It's not like he's back in Nam running recon. His bait piles and fishin' holes are just a few miles from his house, and commander big-shit sends us off in willy-nilly directions to look for him," barked the lady in camo.

"Shit. Who cares? Gray was old," piped in one of the youngest members as he kicked back in his chair holding his Bud Light with both hands.

"Hey!" the militia Sergeant barked and stood up. Everyone in the bar went silent. "Gray was a decorated veteran, who may be a little off, but that's because he risked his life so a sorry-ass punk like you can sit here and drink his cheap, goddamn beer. I suggest you rethink that mister." The Sergeant sat down but continued to stare at the youngster.

Nothing was said, but the boy knew he was wrong as he sat up straight and put his beer on the table.

The buzz of the bar started again.

"Okay, let's just say something happened to Gray. What would it be?" the youngster asked as he tried to make amends with the group.

The oldest man at the table, seventy-year-old Pete Kowalski, took a sip of his Wild Turkey 101, and declared, "He's dead." Then he spit tobacco juice into a Styrofoam cup.

"What?" the woman in camo said as she leaned forward into the group but looked directly at Kowalski.

"He's dead, I said. I've seen your glorious commander talkin' to some slick mother in a big, black Escalade a couple times by the back of the cemetery; my place sits within spittin' distance."

"That don't mean shit," responded camo.

"I also saw Gray arguing with him at the far north end of his property when I was hiking through to the river several weeks ago. I'm tellin' ya, he's dead." His grey beard grabbed as much tobacco juice as the cup he continued to spit into did. Kowalski wiped his mouth with his hand and sipped some more bourbon.

"Why dead?" asked the sergeant.

"Gas."

"Gas?"

"Gas. Can't ya fuckin' hear me?" Kowalski said before he spit again. "Any of you seen the farthest north piece of his property?"

"No," announced the whole table as they looked at each other.

Parker and Sam had barely said a word to each other. Sam was busy writing, and Parker was watching the eleven o'clock news on the TV hanging near the bar—but he hadn't missed a word of the conversation.

The Wild Turkey 101 was gone but Kowalski kept going. "There's some group over on his property line, up the river, test drilling. In fact, between the stand of red and white pines, you'd missed the derrick unless you were right there. Now, it's just a small wellhead with trucks pulling in and out. Gray told me one time there was a slick in the river along his entire frontage—and that's about half a mile."

"Fuck!" exclaimed the sergeant. "That's why the commander steered us into different directions when we were searching for him." He sat back and slumped in his chair. "Shit."

There was a momentary silence at the table.

Parker was thinking about the property for Stanley. Gray's north forty was near the area Parker thought would be the best spot for John Stanley's project. Parker had never ventured toward the river since that land was supposedly protected.

"Sam?" Parker whispered without moving his head. "We need to take a detour home."

"Why?" she said as she continued to write and drink her Kalamazoo-brewed Oberon.

"Don't look around. We need to finish up and take a ride."

"Okay," she whispered back in jest with a smile.

Parker got up from the table and went to the bar to pay the tab. He walked past the table of the militia members twice without notice. Sam wasn't so lucky.

As she stood to leave, Pete Kowalski pointed at Sam, leaned over, spit in his cup, and called, "Hey, you're that woman who was at the hearing!" His voice was more gravelly than before.

"Excuse me, sir." Sam sounded indignant and ready for an argument. "Yes. I was that woman."

No one said anything at the militia table. They looked at each other and waited for someone to comment. Eventually, the Sergeant stood up and held out his hand. "Look, ma'am, we're sorry for treating you the way we did. Is there any way you'd sit and talk with us for a while?"

Parker saw Sam's face soften as the Sergeant extended his hand; nonetheless, he moved between Sam and the militia group.

"Something I can help you folks with?" Parker said with a smile as he towered over everyone. It was one of those times Parker used his height and presence to his advantage.

"It's okay, Parker." Sam gently pulled his shoulder back and moved to accept the greeting from the Sergeant. "You'd really like to talk?" she asked the group as a whole.

"Yes. Well, we think something happened to one of our friends, and we think it might have something to do with what you were talking about. The fracking."

"Yes. Fracking," Sam confirmed.

"Can we talk now?"

"What do you think?" Sam turned to Parker.

"Sure." Parker's ulterior motive was to look at some property in the woods, and it would be easier by himself. "You guys are good, right?" Parker said seriously, with a smile and a wink to the Sergeant, and he put his hand out and firmly shook the Sergeant's hand.

"Yes," the Sergeant said quizzically. "I mean, yes," he said emphatically when he realized Parker wanted to make sure his wife was safe.

"Okay, Sam. I'll be back in an hour."

"Okay, sweetie." She kissed him on the cheek.

Parker pretended to kiss her back but whispered in her ear, "Keep your phone on, in your hand, with the button to call me during the whole meeting."

She pushed him away gently. "I'll be fine. This is huge for me."

Parker hugged her and walked into the cold night. He had his own mystery to solve and trusted Sam with her decision.

"Okay, then folks, how can I help?" Sam asked turning her chair toward their table as they all made room for her. The waitress brought over another round.

Parker drove out of the Swamp's dirt parking lot, over the railroad tracks, and north onto Old US-27. Although he was focused on making John Stanley's legacy work–especially since the check he delivered to Senator Coolridge had gotten the tidal wave moving toward completion, as soon as he turned left onto Cameron Bridge Road and headed west, his mind began to cover different scenarios. What about the well? Why did Gray disappear? Why was John Brooks around? Pat Coruthers and natural gas? John Stanley's desire to put a whole town and region back to work ... what happens if it all collides? Parker's thoughts moved to the Hennessey brothers and his meeting with them at Harborside Deli. How would their lobby efforts progress? Stanley had the governor—or did he? Sir Edward Framingham? The note from Stanley. *This is all connected!* Oil. Gas. The threats and NSA …

He turned right onto Manistee River Road—a dark, teeth-chattering, washboard dirt road—and headed north. The cabins to his left were dark since summer residents had not yet returned. No wildlife. Nothing except blackness. Melting snow splashed against the bottom of the truck in a rhythm made smoother the faster he drove. BAM. The truck hit carve-outs in the road from the snowplows. BAM. The truck rocked and jumped side to side as it hit the holes created from snowmobiles. Finally, he reached the two-track that led back to the river; Parker slowly turned left with only his parking lights on. He drove as far as he could, until a small wooden fence blocked his way. It was old but worked to keep people from driving the last quarter mile to the river. Beyond was the Deward Wildlife Area–a supposedly protected wilderness area.

Since it was one of his favorite kayak entries, Parker knew exactly what was to be expected at the river's edge, where the river turned, and the depth of the water. The path to the river was slushy and rutted from the usual April thaw-and-freeze cycles. Frost was forming, but the air was quiet. With a bright Gibbous moon, he could see well enough to walk without difficulty. He paused before the water and heard a faint, steady hum, almost indiscernible until he tilted his head so one ear faced the direction of the sound and found its proper compass point. He could also hear the river run slowly in front of him as it coursed over deadfalls and rocks. The light snowfall during the winter left the river higher but not rushing as in years past. Parker was taller than it was deep.

He listened. The river gently rolled like a trickling faucet. What was that sound? A generator? A motor of some kind. He didn't carry a flashlight, so he moved slowly. At the canoe launch, knowing Trout Unlimited kept the area meticulously clean, he stepped quietly into the river. The water was frigid against his jeans, but his Merrells gripped well to the river bottom. Mostly sand, there remained wide areas of rock and pebbles. There was more gravel near the headwaters than downstream.

He looked straight ahead, twenty feet. He turned a little south and went around a wing-dam built by the Civilian Conservation Corps under FDR back in the 1930s. Parker began to worry about the muck and marsh that he'd encounter when he reached the opposite bank.

As he neared the edge, the river had become shallow and sand grabbed at his shoes. He took a big step out of the freezing water and right into muck. He struggled to pull his foot out and step forward. Another giant step. He rested and listened. As he stepped, there was a slurping sound as the muck tried to suck him down further. He felt the black particles enter his shoes. Every other step he could feel an old sunken piece of wood or ancient stump. One more giant step, and he was on firm ground. Both feet out; he listened.

He tilted his head again and gave both ears a chance. A faint sound of the river behind him. Still the constancy of a motor humming muffled through the trees. A smell. Natural gas was odorless; this was oil. Burnt oil. And, something else. A chemical taint was in the air.

The first row of trees was cedar. Their soft, full needles brushed against his Mountain Hardwear coat. The stiff branches of the undergrowth grabbed at him. He moved through the alder branches and empty tamaracks. A game path was at his feet as he traversed through rows of red pines. In the moonlight, he could see a sheen pooled in the melting snow. Parker was concentrating and his focus was heightened for sounds and smells. He began to see faint light through breaks in the thicker spruce and hemlocks as the forest changed, and in another ten minutes of slowly walking his cover broke.

John Mansfield was in his office after another missed dinner. His cardigan sweater was a mess and his tie hung on the back of a chair in front of him.

"Yes, ma'am. We continue to look. We're now in all fifty states looking, listening, and reading legislative hearings and filings to check changes. Uh-huh. Yes, but not enough data for conclusions at this point. Yes, ma'am. I will. Thank you. Good night."

He set his phone down and looked at the old paper map that only he continued to use. Pins were everywhere, from small towns in North Dakota to Turkmenistan. The circle on the map around Frederic, Michigan, was the newest mystery. He stood and walked around his desk, picking up another phone that was on his office table. He punched in a number and someone in Azerbaijan answered.

# TWENTY-ONE

PARKER STOOD CONCEALED BEHIND A GRACIOUS WHITE pine that probably started growing prior to the Civil War and somehow had missed the axe. He stared at something he'd only seen in Sam's research of test areas for fracking. The generator was suddenly loud. Lights, strategically placed like a baseball field, directed down and toward the middle of the clearing; all set within a wall of old-growth white pines, spruce, and red pines. "Gray *is* dead," Parker whispered to himself.

He turned quietly to walk along the tree line by the fracking well, inching his way through pine boughs. He was careful to avoid the cameras he noticed around the perimeter. Getting any closer wouldn't change what he saw; he'd seen enough. It was time to retrieve Sam and return home.

Turning around to his left with his head down to avoid a fallen tree, Parker suddenly felt a thud against the side of his head. His left ear was somewhere between ringing and deaf. The thicket of dead branches below the canopy stuck out from the tree trunks, and he felt one tear into his side as he fell. Eyes closed, he tried to open them and collect himself. Instantly he thought early bear. His right ear was working and he heard twigs breaking; then realized he wasn't moving. From his knees, he rose quickly as he opened his eyes and saw the hulk of a man romping toward him.

Parker lowered himself like a linebacker breaking down to tackle a fullback head-on. He caught the man's midsection and drove him back through a thicket of jack pine. Branches cracked as loud as the man groaned. Losing his wind from Parker's shoulder ramming his lower sternum and diaphragm, the man hurdled backward.

Keeping his fists clenched, Parker wrapped his arms around the massive midsection of his assailant and could feel the dead pine branches cutting into his knuckles. He drove the man downward into the mud and slush. There was a loud thud; Parker could feel the vibration of the ground and the air leaving the man's lungs. He was afraid he'd killed him. Parker looked at the large, older man. His eyes were closed and face grimaced, but more importantly, Parker could feel air return to the man's chest.

The bright moon showed only a glint of snowpack under the trees, but it was enough to expose a path. Parker pushed hard on the chest of his attacker to make sure he lost air again, then he launched himself forward through the woody undergrowth and disappeared into the forest. His adrenaline didn't allow for pain. Parker made a quick glance back to see that no one was following.

Knowing the area like he did, Parker ran east. He needed to get to the river to make better sense of where he was. He paused to listen. Only the low hum of the generator and pumps. The forest was dark behind him.

Keeping a quick and steady pace, Parker found the river and immediately got his bearings. One foot into the deep muck; then the other. A shorter distance to water, but as he heard and felt the sucking sound of the soft blackness around his right lower leg behind him, the frigid water stung his left leg in front. He'd stepped into a deep hole along the current of an outside backflow. The water was up to his neck as his rear leg exited the muck. The cold startled him out of the fog he hadn't realized enveloped him after the blow. A quick shake of his head and some deep breaths, and he was out of the hole in two steps. The water, now ankle deep, allowed him to take four long strides to the eastern bank. The fishing path along the river going south took him directly to the Trout Unlimited area where he'd originally entered.

*Sam!* he thought. Then he caught himself. *She'll be okay.* His hands resting on his knees, dripping wet, he lifted his head to look and listen for anything beyond the soft, gurgling stream. Nothing.

Pain. Stabbing and throbbing pain. The adrenaline was wearing off. He hurt below his ribs on his right side. He brought his left hand up and over to feel. A stick was embedded in his flesh deep enough to hurt but fortunately it hadn't broken through to any vital areas.

Parker could feel the wet and cold take over his body. Paradoxically, the relief of being close to his truck calmed him. Once there, he reached up under the left front fender, grabbed the key he had set on top of the tire, and opened the door. The Swiss Army knife in his faithful backpack was easily accessible. He shut off the dome light and sat against the right front tire, away from the river. His small flashlight held close to the wound provided enough ambient light to cut skin and pull the wood out clean.

"Shit! Sonovabitch!" Parker quietly yelled.

He knocked the back of his head against the fender which immediately reminded him the left side of his head was throbbing. He felt around his left ear; the warmth of the blood was exaggerated against the cold of his fingers. The blood was now trickling down his left cheek and his neck. There was already a crust formed from earlier blood; and although he wasn't dizzy, the fog was returning to his thought process but not enough to dim the desire of getting back to Sam safely. Parker reached forward and gathered some snow to put up along his temple. He instantly felt the cold and the searing pain. The lump was palpable. More deep breaths, then Parker stood up slowly and got into the truck.

His cell phone showed no signal. He turned off the automatic headlights, started the engine, and quickly tapped the brakes to release the transmission. He felt his clothes squish water onto the seat as he shivered. He drove the truck southeast out onto Manistee River Road and turned on the headlights. He looked in the rearview mirror. Nothing.

Anger gnawed at him. The throbbing in his head stopped as a new round of adrenaline was pumped into his system. He had to trust Sam was okay.

He flew down the dirt roads, hydroplaning over the washboard surface. Once on pavement, it took seconds to get to 80 mph. In no time, he was sliding into the Swamp's dirt lot. Without even thinking about what he looked like, Parker jumped out of the truck. His heavy, wet clothes slowed him, along with the return of the throbbing pain in his left temple and under his right ribs. He took a few running steps—no, that wasn't going to work. Gasping, he caught the handle of the Swamp's front door and held it momentarily before opening it. He shut his eyes and hoped that Sam was okay. He stepped inside.

"Holy shit, honey! What happened to you?"

Parker held it together enough to walk to the bar using his best David Niven impression—straight, firm, and as if nothing was wrong. Sam was still at the round table with about twenty people listening to her. It was like Queen Elizabeth and her court. Parker stood straight as he ordered. Sam returned her attention to the group, but they all stared at Parker dripping like the creature from the black lagoon.

"Dewars. Double and neat." Parker tried to act like he was a normal customer.

The bartender couldn't take his eyes off Parker. The sight of a six-five, two-hundred-fifty-pound man standing at the bar, dripping blood from his temple and water from the rest of his body, wasn't even normal for Frederic on a bad day. Parker drank the scotch and slammed down the empty glass. He turned around to see Sam walking over. He looked down and realized he was standing in a pool of water as muck and blood dripped on the floor.

"Parker?" The closer Sam got to him, the more alarmed she became. "PARKER?"

"Yes?" he said as if nothing were wrong. The David Niven thing again.

"What the hell happened?" Sam grasped his arm at the elbow.

"Nothing, why?" Parker said dryly.

"You're bleeding. You're a mess—Parker, don't tell me nothing."

"Oh, this?" Parker looked at his clothing and then held up his empty glass to the bartender. "I got attacked."

"Attacked?" Sam was wide-eyed as she sat on a barstool next to Parker. The crowd was conversing among themselves back at the large, round table.

"Yes." He grabbed Sam by her right elbow and walked her to the far end of the bar, away from everyone. He stopped and pulled a chair out for Sam to sit at a table. "I went to Gray's north forty—it's across the river from the land I was proposing for John Stanley. There's some kind of well set up and there's a pipe in the river where they are pumping water, and there's enough chemicals in the snow to make the place glow at night." Parker looked over Sam at the crowd of people to make sure they weren't wandering toward them. "And just as I was leaving the site, some big fuck tries to take me out."

"What happened to him?" Sam was listening intently while looking at Parker as if he was a sideshow at a circus.

"Last time I saw him, he was flat on his back." Parker winced but didn't know whether to grab his head or his side. He drank the other glass of scotch.

"Parker, where are you hurt?" Sam rubbed his hair with her right hand and his cheek with her left hand.

"There was a stick in my side, but it's out. My head got hit with something." He felt the lump. "Can we just go?" Parker was attempting his best David Niven, but he looked more like someone from a bad day on the Discovery Channel.

"Sure. Sure." Sam walked over to the group at the round table.

"Is everything okay?" asked the Sergeant.

"Yes. Parker had an accident, but he'll be fine. Can we continue this discussion at the next public forum they're having here?" Sam was almost pleading. She knew she had to get Parker out of there, but they really wanted to learn more about fracking.

"Yes, ma'am. We'll be here."

"Great. I'll see you then." Sam turned back toward Parker. She laid cash on the bar for his drinks as she ushered him outside to the truck.

It was almost closing time when he staggered into the Swamp, arching his back with his right hand pushing in on his lumbar area. His clothes were torn and wet.

"Holy shit, Commander! What happened to you?" the Sergeant asked.

"Don't ask. Hey, Ray, give me a triple and bring it over to my table." The Commander of the local militia walked to his usual seat by the pool table.

No one from the large, round table offered to help the Commander; they just watched him sit in quiet indignation. Pete Kowalski was the last one to get up to leave. He spit the last of his tobacco into the white cup, set it on a table near the door, turned around and looked at the Commander, shook his head, and then followed the others.

# TWENTY-TWO

ON THE OTHER SIDE OF THE WORLD, IT WAS A RARE meeting of all ten members of the RFA. They were sitting in their favorite spots, while brunch was served. Sir Edward sat in the middle of the longest sofa, with his right arm resting atop the back cushion and his left hand cavorting with his favorite Hendricks gin. He watched everyone chatting.

"Good morning. I wanted to thank you all for attending on such short notice. We have some updates we felt would be best done in person. Evgeny, if you please."

"Da. We have had a security issue you should all be made aware of. A contracted person became a liability; so a change has been made. And we have shut down all communication connected to RFA everywhere in the world."

"Thus, my flying in and out of places," Sir Edward interjected. "Continue, sir."

"We must remain quiet for a length of time. Please, your patience."

"Ingrid?" Sir Edward pointed to his Norwegian colleague.

"Yes. We made all appropriate donations before the difficulty arose. The accounts have been quiet and stand in reserve. Some groups in the United States are calling for legislation or rules to extrapolate donors from the super PACs. Much of our money went to fight those indignations. We also cornered the market in India on guar gum."

"What? Guar gum?" asked a member sitting next to her.

"Yes. It's essential in keeping the drilled openings from closing as they are made during the process of hydraulic fracturing. Our engineers alerted us that the market price was skyrocketing."

"Thank you, Ingrid. Nazar?" Sir Edward gestured his glass toward his always suspicious friend from Turkmenistan.

"All oil and gas exploration continues to expand. The agreed upon profit percentage was front loaded into RFA to assure quiet accounts for the interim. No loss of momentum. All within the United States continues to expand. Buried in the lease and legislative agenda of Michigan is language that provides us access to all 57,000 square miles." He paused and smiled. "And, most importantly, the water! Sir Edward's own U.K. is now contemplating a reversal on the fracking ban. Thank you to Sir Edward's influence." Nazar, with his perfect Oxford accent, was honored to be the political watchman for the group after his last meeting with Sir Edward.

"Excellent, Nazar. Now, please, eat." Sir Edward stood and walked to the edge of the circle of sofas and chairs where the group sat. He finished his gin and set it on a tray held by a server. After straightening his suit, he cleared his throat. "I wanted to ask the opinion of the group about offering a spot to an American. After all, the boom is the biggest miracle to hit places like North Dakota since gold in California."

Evgeny purposely did not look at anyone; instead he concentrated on his eggs benedict. He was the only person who was aware of the attempt to recruit John Stanley.

The group murmured and chatted. Finally, Ingrid spoke. "Sir Edward, with all due respect, we believe it to be an unwise choice. We will say no more."

"Right," Sir Edward grabbed another Hendricks from the server standing next to him. "I shall forget the idea and make no mention of it again. Now, let us relax and enjoy each other's company until our departures." He sat down and began to eat without losing his smile. He glanced over at Evgeny who was smiling back.

"Za zdorovie!" Evgeny raised his glass of vodka and gestured with a toast to Sir Edward.

† † †

"John, Sir Edward has been flying all over the globe, and yet we can't find anything going on around him. You?" John Mansfield was sitting back with his feet on the desk crossed at the ankles. It was close to 3:00 a.m.

"Man, John, I'm tired. Not a peep in Grand Rapids or from Anakova. He's vanished into thin air."

"Well, you know about that. It's what spooks do."

"Yeah, but you wanna be better than the other guy."

"So, let's get you home and figure the next move." Mansfield was now up and putting his cardigan on the door hook and grabbing his coat.

"Your call, boss. Pellston, tomorrow?"

"Yup. I'll send the plane. Oh, and John, Ramsey says hello."

Sam and Parker were in their favorite spot after having adventures: reading in bed. Neither could sleep, even though it was 3:30 a.m.

"Sam, I know the physics of fracking, but what's the true fear?" Parker was reviewing some of her group's literature.

"I'll make you a deal. I'll tell you if you find me a path around the legislature and governor."

"Deal." Parker was still in pain from the ten stitches in his side after their visit to the emergency room in Petoskey. Sam had insisted he be seen by a doctor.

"The fear comes from several parts. One, the chemicals in the water can leak through the cement-lined wells into other open aquifers or old wells, and it gets poorly handled at the surface."

"So, that's what causes the slicks in the river and all over the snow?"

"Yes. The pipe from the river may allow for use of fewer trucks, making the area less traveled, but they still need to provide for the chemicals."

"There were some huge tanks and motors pumping."

"Sounds like this group has money to find new and better ways to frack. The other worry for us in Michigan is our freshwater. As you know, the Great Lakes are the largest source of freshwater in the world. Can you imagine if our thirst for energy goes beyond our wish for water?"

"Proven problems?"

"Everywhere. The taint is money and politics. Even at the University of Texas, a lead investigator who found fracking safe was sitting on the board of Plains Exploration and Production Company. The University pulled the study results but not until after more money was sent in favor of fracking."

"Small earthquakes where they were not expected?"

"Fracking."

"Poisoned wells where there was no reason for one?"

"Fracking. Just because the wellhead is a mile away doesn't mean the drill didn't take a left turn for another mile."

"And England?"

"Bought-and-paid-for politicians see an end to Middle East oil, fine, but at what expense? We believe we should use less fossil fuel or find other ways to make energy?"

"Your answers really do convince. Haven't worked anywhere, eh?"

"Nope. One last shot at it with ole' Dutch Van Der Knacht in Frederic. Now, it's your turn."

"Elementary, my dear Watson. Elementary." Parker's pain was subsiding. Vicodin does that. He kissed Sam on the cheek and reached over to shut out his light. Sam grabbed him back.

"Not so fast, swamp boy."

*The elders felt powerless to lead the others through the tumultuous times and change in the homeland. In Turkmenistan and Azerbaijan, there were not many choices for the locals. As capitalism was brought to the people, there became a strange mix of tribal cultures satisfied with what they have, those that enjoyed the new materialism, and young men and women confusing ancient roles of gender. Their lands had disappeared under the ideal of "economic growth"—but at what cost to their way of life? The elders watched what happened in the West. No matter the wealth and desires of the people, the richest capitalist gets what he wants.*

# TWENTY-THREE

FRIDAY, APRIL 22

THE MORNING WAS BRIGHT BUT CHILLY. SAM WOKE UP disgruntled, even after a nice romantic night once the lights went out. She woke up mumbling something about a Leadership Team meeting at work and pecked Parker on the cheek before she left.

Parker was sitting with a cup of coffee, looking out over the lake. He wasn't actively avoiding her before she left, but his preoccupation with the call he was making gave him an easy out.

"John, can we meet tonight?"

"Sure. The New York around eight?" John Stanley replied.

"Make it nine. I have some business to take care of. See you then."

Parker put his phone down and continued to hatch the plot to make Sam a hero, or at least in a better mood.

It wasn't until late afternoon that Pat Coruthers was in his black Escalade driving north on US-31 through Charlevoix on a venture to secure the insurance on further fracking now that the state legislature was certain to finalize the leases. He hadn't heard anything more from the Chicago law firm after Bob Clauson went missing. With the FBI now involved in the missing person complaint, Coruthers ended the relationship after making sure Clauson hadn't said anything about the detour to assist with Anakova. The firm was aware only of the trip to visit properties and then Clauson just up and disappeared. Coruthers had received a personal call from Sir Edward to inform him all was safe and quiet.

Coruthers was in the mood to get away with his wife and son. The boat was already in the water at Bay Harbor, and even though it might stay docked, a nice trip with the family would ensure a release from the pressure.

ť ť ť

The plane was at Pellston Airport as scheduled. John Brooks secured his car in the new hangar that most still believed was built for maintenance and emergency equipment. As the plane made its way to Langley AFB, Brooks couldn't get Dimitri Anakova out of his mind. Why had he vanished? The FBI was searching for the attorney whose car turned up empty. The only prints found were Clauson's. NSA wasn't volunteering anything.

A text came in on his personal phone. It was from Parker Moore.

**We have to talk. Tomorrow!**

*Now what?* Brooks wondered. Tim Johnson had said all was quiet, and the only remarkable event from the Grayling area was a natural gas explosion of an old mobile home. Apparently a crazy, old militia member was careless. Brooks didn't answer the text. He'd wait.

ť ť ť

"Parker, we have some bad news and some good news. Which first?" Rance Hennessey was calling from the brothers' Lansing office a block from the Capitol on North Seymour Street.

"Bad." Parker was driving to Cava for some quiet writing time before they opened. He wanted a change of venue–but one with Lagavulin. His bottle was empty.

"The property you had us working on is off limits. No reason given."

"Figured," Parker said softly.

"What's that?" Rance asked.

"Nothing. What else?"

"We did find a great piece of land on both sides of the railroad tracks, with Old US-27 right in the middle and, best of all, I-75 on the east end." Rance waited to make sure they had correctly guessed Parker and John Stanley's desire.

"Hennessey, that's perfect. The timing is even better."

"Good." Rance Hennessey gave a thumbs-up to Lance, who was sitting across the room in a plush, dark-burgundy leather chair by the fireplace. "Good." Rance sat back in his swivel desk chair and lit a cigar.

"Can you secure it?" As Parker was pulling into Cava's rear parking lot, he spotted Pat Coruthers's black Escalade exit the gated Peninsula Drive.

"Already did, Mr. Moore. Already did," exclaimed Rance with the cigar in his mouth. He was trying to do his best FDR impersonation.

After dropping off his wife and son at the largest home on Peninsula Drive in Bay Harbor, Pat Coruthers drove into Petoskey and parked in front of Chandler's. It was time to finalize the insurance deal; then he could relax. He walked into the restaurant and surveyed the surroundings. Six of the ten tables were full, but the two-top against the back wall was awaiting him.

"Dinner or drinks this afternoon?" Rich came around from behind the bar to greet Pat.

"I believe my secretary made a reservation. Coruthers?"

"Let me check." Rich turned to glance at the Open Table screen on the monitor. "Here we are. Table five. Right this way."

The restaurant was an intimate spot with little room for maneuvering between the entrance, tables, and bar. As a destination fine-food establishment, most customers liked the charm and accepted the congestion. Samuals was seated at the end of the bar near where Rich and Coruthers stood and thus overheard their conversation. Having never met before, Samuals stood and stepped between the two.

"Mr. Coruthers?" Samuals stuck out his right hand. "I'm Don Samuals."

"Ah, yes. Mr. Samuals. Shall we continue at the table?"

The two made their way to table five and sat. Coruthers asked for a Dewars and water as Paul took over for Rich who had a phone call.

"Yeah," Rich said into the phone. "Yup. Just walked in. Okay, it's your funeral."

Parker was sitting in Cava nursing a snifter of Lagavulin after putting his phone in his pocket. He was perched over his journal with his left elbow on the bar and the left cheek of his face resting in his hand; he slowly ran his right index finger around the rim of the glass. He'd only written half a paragraph while listening to Diana Krall in her torch-singer best and looking through the far windows at two boats sitting quietly in the sheltered harbor.

Jette stood inside the triangular-shaped bar with her back to Parker. She was cutting lemons and limes for the soon-to-be arriving drinkers. The servers and chefs were busy getting everything set for the dinner patrons since Cava opened at 5:00 p.m., later than the eateries in Petoskey. The restaurant usually didn't fill until after 7:00 p.m.

"Jette?" Parker said.

"What's up, Parker?" Jette didn't turn around. She continued to slice.

"Shit." Parker gazed out the windows at the boats.

"That's dark, Parker."

"Shitty people, Jette. Shitty people."

"Trouble?" Jette finally turned and her blonde hair fell around her face and shoulders. The blue eyes centered on Parker.

"Some."

"Bobby helping?" She always seemed to know what Bobby was doing.

"Part. The rest is up to me." Parker hadn't moved. He did stop rimming the snifter and took a sip. "Somebody's tried to kill me three times in seven years. I can deal with that. But don't go after my wife." He sat up straight, broadened his chest and shoulders, and with some effort, took a deep breath against his stitches.

"Here." Jette poured more of the pungent single malt. "I don't know how you drink that shit, Parker. Did you get a ride or did you drive?"

"Drove."

"Sam?"

"Mad."

"You?"

"Not sure."

"Need a place?"

"No. Time."

Three people showed up at the bar. Regulars Jette didn't mind seeing. They tipped well. It was a brunette with two guys older than she; one on each hip, then on each side of her at the bar. Money brought out the best trophy stock. She rubbed one man on the thigh and the other on the face as she smiled. Jette set three glasses of wine before them without them having to say a word; then she walked back and leaned on the bar in front of Parker and rolled her eyes.

"Jette, as a woman, you like heroes or sensitive?"

"Depends."

"On?"

"Time of day. Time of month. Circumstances."

"Heroes?" Parker asked, after he downed the scotch.

"Usually."

"Sam needs a hero." Parker glared at the trophy and her polishers.

"You be da' man, Parker." Jette moved the empty snifter.

Parker thought momentarily. He reached into his pocket and pulled out a hundred dollar bill and put it on the counter. He looked at Jette. She looked back, perplexed, with her blonde hair and blue eyes tilted to one side.

"First of all, Parker, you never carry money, so that's probably counterfeit. Second, I wouldn't take it anyways."

"Am I that predictable?" Parker said sarcastically. "It's real. You keep it." He was pushing away from the bar. "Besides, you know, people do pay me for my brain."

She grabbed the bill and put it in the pocket of her tight, black slacks.

"We sure don't. We like you for your size."

"Dream on, Jette." Parker had his back to the bar and was walking toward the front door. He waved with the back of his hand. "Dream on."

"Moore?" Jette yelled.

Parker stopped and turned around just as he began to push the door open.

"Be careful," Jette said as she wiped the bar.

Parker paused, winked, then lowered his head and walked out.

# TWENTY-FOUR

THE TWO MEN AT TABLE FIVE DISCUSSED THEIR BUSINESS as people came and went around them. Their quiet conversation drew no attention, and no one in the restaurant recognized them.

"The policy?" Samuals took a drink of his Ketel One and ice cascaded toward his mouth. He set down the glass with an indignant stare at Coruthers.

"All is in order. Our legal department reviewed it and said we were good to go." Coruthers was calm and collected.

"Check or cash?" Samuals asked.

"Cash."

"Tonight?" Samuals was surprised.

"No. I'll have it delivered to any location you choose tomorrow."

Before Samuals could answer, Coruthers looked up and watched Parker Moore walk in and take a seat at the edge of the bar near the front door.

"Coffee," Parker said to Rich.

"Irish?" Rich asked.

"No. You'll know when."

Rich smiled and brought over a white mug of coffee.

"Excuse me," Coruthers said to Samuals as he stood up and walked over to the bar. His gait was confident and steady, and he never took his eyes off of Parker.

Don Samuals turned to watch.

"Moore?" Coruthers stood behind Parker and waited for him to turn around.

"Coruthers." Parker didn't move.

After a moment of silence, Pat Coruthers put his right hand on Parker's right shoulder. Still no movement.

Silence.

"Moore. It's me, Pat Coruthers. How are you?" Coruthers said with a smile, trying to be the chum and get past the embarrassment of no response while people watched.

Without a hint of intention, Parker grabbed Coruthers's hand, exploded off of the bar stool, and twisted the surprised man's wrist behind him. The next thing Coruthers saw was the bar coming rapidly toward his face. The wooden bar squeaked a little as Coruthers's face slid a couple inches when his right cheek was planted firmly into the wet. His left hand and arm were clinched awkwardly behind his back. He grunted in pain, but couldn't move against Parker's size and strength.

Most everyone in Chandler's knew Parker. No one moved. The few who didn't know Parker took their cue from those who did. Don Samuals quickly became interested in his own drink and stared at the back wall of the restaurant away from the bar, wishing he could disappear into the woodwork.

"I saw your Escalade outside, Coruthers. Where's your other one?" Parker was whispering into Coruthers's left ear.

No response.

"If I see another truck like yours around my house, my wife, or my cats, I'm coming to Grand Rapids and do this in an alley where you won't walk out. You hear me, Mr. Coruthers?" Parker wanted to invoke the name of Sir Edward, but stopped. He didn't want all of his cards on the table.

"I got it, Moore, but I don't think you understand what you're getting into." Coruthers spoke out of the left side of his mouth.

"Coruthers, you have no idea what the fuck I can get into." Parker twisted his arm ever so slightly.

"Will you kindly let me go? I will press charges."

"You don't have any witnesses."

"There's an entire restaurant watching."

"Anyone see anything?" Parker looked around the room as Samuals exited quietly.

Silence.

"I don't think anyone will believe your story. So, again, I see a black Escalade anywhere around anyone I know, and I'm coming after you." Parker twisted Coruthers' arm until it almost broke, then released his grip.

As Coruthers stood and gathered himself and wiped the moisture off his face with a bar napkin, he surveyed the room. No one looked at him.

Finally, Rich caught his eye and winked. "Don't worry, sir. We'll pick up your tab."

Parker stood as tall and as wide as his two-hundred-and-fifty-pound, six-foot-five-inch-frame allowed. He stood a foot away from Coruthers and stared down at him. No one made a sound. Coruthers put the napkin on the bar and walked quickly out the door.

"Now," Parker said as he sat back on his stool.

The restaurant began a conversational buzz, with much of it laughter.

Outside Coruthers slithered into his black Escalade. He sped away, glaring out the windshield as if the town sheriff in Dodge City had told him to skedaddle.

Rich poured the Jamison into Parker's coffee. "Parker, what are you, anyway?"

"I'm a poet and a writer," Parker said, looking up.

"Bullshit."

# TWENTY-FIVE

"HELLO, MR. STANLEY," SAID BILL MILLER, THE DINING room manager at the New York in Harbor Springs. "Can I have Joe bring your usual? No olives."

"That would be fine, Bill. Have him pour a snifter of Laphroaig as well. The ten-year." John Stanley was wearing his best Brooks Brothers'.

"Yes, sir." Bill motioned for Stephanie, who ran over from the back upper-level dining room. The New York was a classic harbor-side steakhouse; a quaint place for a drink or a formal dinner. The ambiance hadn't changed since it originally opened in 1904.

"Table 25 for Mr. Stanley and ...?" Bill looked at his best guest.

"Mr. Moore. Parker Moore will be joining me."

"Very good. Table 25 for two, Stephanie."

"Right this way, Mr. Stanley," Stephanie said nervously. A billionaire customer caused that type of reaction.

"Stephanie," Stanley said as they walked downstairs to the private dining room known as Table 25, "knowing my friend, he'll be hungry. Could you please have the cornmeal-crusted oysters accompany the scotch?"

"Absolutely. I'll have Joe order both. Now, sir?" Stephanie stepped aside as John Stanley slowly entered the Gatsbyesque room.

"How about in fifteen minutes? Moore is never on time."

"Yes, sir. Thank you, sir." Stephanie looked down as Stanley handed her a hundred dollar bill.

As Stephanie stepped back into the main dining room, Parker Moore entered. He was rubbing the top of his head as if he was trying to wake up.

"Can I help you?" Bill said as he looked at Parker with a suspicious eye. He wasn't used to seeing people in jeans and a tattered tweed coat.

"Ah, I believe John Stanley's waiting for me?"

"You— I mean, yes. Stephanie?" Bill tried to act polite. "Take …" he looked back at Parker and gazed at him up and down. "… this gentleman to Table 25."

"Him?" Stephanie asked softly.

"Him," Bill said quietly.

"Um, right this way, sir," begged a hesitant Stephanie as she led Parker past the bar and down the stairs to Table 25.

"Moore. Dressed to the nines, I see." Stanley sipped his martini sans olives. He didn't get up.

"Go easy on me, John. Been an interesting day–and night."

"Obviously. That'll be all, Stephanie. I can handle it from here."

"Stephanie?" Parker sat across the table as Stephanie shut the door. "John, I need you to call Sir Edward and accept the invitation to his group."

"Why?"

"Because I have a friend who'd be very interested in having you on the inside."

Stephanie knocked.

"It's okay, Stephanie. Please."

She set a plate of six oysters and the Laphroaig in front of Parker.

"You don't look like a Stephanie," Parker said.

Stephanie just smiled and left. *Asshole*, she thought as she shut the door.

"Now, about your friend, Parker?" John Stanley sat with his elbows on the table and his hands clasped in front of his face. He had no idea what was about to unfold.

A couple hours later, Sam and Parker were reading in bed. Parker was re-reading Faulkner's *The Sound and the Fury* while Sam read the day's *Petoskey News & Review*.

Parker yawned.

"A purpose. I want to make a difference," Sam muttered.

"What?" Parker looked over to his right.

"A difference." Sam put down the paper.

"You are. Us."

"Come on, Parker. You know what I mean. You have a legacy; people still enjoy lives changed by things you've done. Me? I make paper. I shuffle paper. I shred paper. I …"

"Stop," Parker interrupted. He grabbed her and pulled her over to him.

She relaxed.

"I just want to make a difference."

"You will, Sam. You will," Parker said, clutching Sam's head to his chest as he grimaced from the pressure on his stitched wound. He looked past her and knew he was on the right path.

*The National Security Agency had the world wired, but with only a few NSA agents, that meant the CIA had to do most of the fieldwork—although the NSA made sure the people it did plant around the world were well hidden. Big Brother did exist—sometimes under one's own nose.*

# TWENTY-SIX

SATURDAY, APRIL 23

PARKER WAS SITTING QUIETLY IN TIM JOHNSON'S OFFICE. He'd called Parker at 6:30 a.m. and urged his appearance.

"So, I got a call late last night from a lawyer in Grand Rapids. They would like to have me investigate a disturbance in Chandler's yesterday."

"Yeah?" Parker was drinking coffee from the Roast & Toast.

"Yes. Am I going to find there was a disturbance?" Johnson was looking at the message from the attorney.

"Probably not."

"Okay." Johnson crumpled the piece of paper and tossed it into the wastebasket. He swiveled his chair and looked out the window at the lake.

"Hypothetically … ?" Parker said as he looked out the same window.

"Hypothetically …" Johnson replied, not moving his gaze.

"If someone was following your wife, parking outside your house, had someone blow up a trailer around you, and showed up in town trying to make nice, like nothing happened, would you say something to him?"

"Hypothetically?" Johnson repeated, still looking out the window.

"Hypothetically." Parker agreed, still looking out the window.

"I'd find out what his business was; then I'd kick his ass—hypothetically."

"Okay, then." Parker stood up to leave. Just as he reached the doorway, Johnson stopped him.

"Parker, I don't know what's going on yet, but you're on a short leash."

After turning around, Parker smiled. "Give me a couple days. I'm heading to Lansing."

"Sam and the house?" Johnson had swung his chair around and was leaning on his desk with both elbows.

"Do you mind?" Parker asked as he stood in the doorway.

"No. We'll watch. Be careful."

Parker knocked on the wooden doorjamb three times with his fist, turned, and walked away.

ɾ ɾ ɾ

John Stanley placed the call, as he promised Parker he would. His house on Harbor Point was cool in the spring and quiet since he was the first and only resident who had returned to the exclusive summertime hangout for the wealthy. The waves lapped onto the sandy Lake Michigan beach below his bay window. This was the view he wanted for his death. A quiet moment in his favorite room. He hoped his jet-set family would take the time to be with him near the end. Stanley's ambition and fortune made for a lonely life–something he had not anticipated.

The number he tried was out of service. *Strange*, he thought. It was the number he kept on his phone from Sir Edward's first call. He dialed a different number. "Jane? Can you get me Sir Edward Framingham's office in London? Thanks. Just connect the call when you find him. Thanks, Jane."

ɾ ɾ ɾ

Mansfield sat in his office contemplating the day's news. HSBC was fined $1.9 billion by the U.S. Justice Department for laundering money for drug cartels and terror groups–the information his staff had provided to the CIA, FBI, and Justice. Now his staff was searching for the Resources For All accounts that had disappeared into the mist. The intelligence was coming together but not fast enough. The politics and interest around oil and gas was quicker.

The President of the United States was in a bind. The energy pendulum was swinging in his favor but at what cost? Over $12 million had been dispersed to federal candidates from oil and gas in the last election, with eighty-seven percent going to the GOP. No surprise, but it was directly donated to the candidates. There was still no accounting for the undisclosed money used by the super PACs. The super PAC filings would be coming out this quarter, but only for the public to be able to see what they thought was the reality. Dark money under Citizen's United was still dark money the public never saw.

The phone call to Azerbaijan was productive and the plan was going according to schedule.

A knock on his half open door.

"Hey, chief." John Brooks walked in.

"John. Good to see you. Shut the door and come in." Mansfield came from behind his desk and they both sat at the table that was strewn with books and maps.

"You know, boss, computers, tablets, and smart phones can hold all of this info for you. This looks like a Jurassic-era office."

"It works for me. Look, we need to get Parker Moore on speaker. You said there was a message from him wanting to talk. Let's call him together."

"K. Now?"

"Now."

"Rance, you guys still down in Lansing?" Parker was on the phone early for a Saturday, but he knew Rance and Lance would be up and running and at the ready.

"Are you kidding? With this anti-union legislation being rammed through, we're so busy our heads are spinning."

"Can you get me a meeting with the governor? A private meeting?" Parker was sitting at Center City Gym awaiting a client. He continued to do some personal training on the side to keep himself in shape. He watched the people and cars pass back and forth in front of the windows that spanned the length of the gym on Mitchell Street.

"Wait. I got a call on the office phone. Talk to Lance." Rance Hennessey handed the phone to his brother.

"What's up, Moore?" Lance asked.

"I need you to get me a meeting with the governor."

"Now?"

"Now." Parker heard another call coming into his cell. "I have to go. I have another call, but call me with a date and time. Hello?" Parker didn't try to look at the number, but it didn't matter. It was restricted.

"Moore. John Mansfield. I've got John Brooks with me. Can you get to Tim Johnson's office?"

"Ah, sure." Parker had to take a second and reconnect with the world after realizing who was on the phone. "I can be there in five minutes."

"Good. He knows you're coming."

"Got it." Parker put his phone in his pocket, and looked over at the owner of Center City Gym. "Mark, can you let Mr. Pascal know I had to cancel?" Parker was not rushing, but there was purpose in every movement as he gathered up his gym bag and journal. He was almost out the door.

"Sure, Parker. What should I tell him?" Mark asked from behind the front counter.

"Tell him I had an emergency and will call tomorrow."

Parker walked west on Mitchell Street as he made his way to the Department of Public Safety on Lake Street west of US-31.

Sam had gone into her office to work in the quiet of the weekend. After copying all of her notes and testimony from past fracking hearings, she locked her office and headed around town to pick up her friends for the next act of the Dutch Van Der Knacht show at the Swamp in Frederic. She'd promised Parker she would not go alone.

"Hello, Cindy. I guess the boss is expecting me?" Parker stood calmly at the front desk of the Petoskey Public Safety office.

"Hold on, Parker. He's been busy today, and I don't want to piss him off any more than I have to." Cindy picked up the phone. "Chief, Parker Moore for you. Sure." She hung up. "He wants you in the dispatch room downstairs." Cindy was writing on a sticky note. "Here. He told me to give you the code."

"Thanks, Cindy. I'll eat it after I use it."

"Makes no matter to me, Moore," she said turning back to her computer screen. "I think half the town knows it." Cindy said softly to herself.

Parker made his way down the stairs and into the basement. Dispatch was as it should be for a well-to-do, sophisticated, small police department. Monitors, phones, computers, wires, and large screens on the walls filled the area—but without the Hollywood lighting and women sitting around in low-cut shirts and tight pants.

"Moore, over here." Johnson waved Parker into a side room with a small window in the door. "Guess you're not going to Lansing just yet."

Parker walked by the three staff in uniform taking calls and working the computers. During the night, the room would be empty since all dispatch went through a central countywide system at the county building a few blocks away.

"In here, Parker. This is the most secure line. They're going to dial in a couple minutes. What the hell you been doin' out there? It's not every day I get a call from Fort Meade and the NSA." Johnson was making his way into one of four chairs around a small wood-and-metal table. "I knew it was about you as soon as I knew who they were." He sat and readied a legal pad and pen.

"Well," Parker was already sitting on the other side of the table. The speaker phone was in the middle of the table. He took a deep breath. "I guess we'll hear what they have to say."

The speaker phone buzzed.

"Johnson here."

"Director. John Mansfield and John Brooks. Is Parker in attendance?"

"Yes, he is." Johnson looked up from the speaker at Parker.

"Hey, guys," Parker said gazing down at the speaker.

Speaker phones were interesting. People always stared into them as if the people on both sides could see each other. NSA had that capability, but Petoskey dispatch wasn't there yet.

"Parker. John Brooks here. Good to hear your voice."

"Yeah. Except you've been around me for a week. What the hell?" Parker wasn't perturbed, but his voice was close.

"Fieldwork, Parker. We think Sir Edward's group is up and running again and fracking is the new front," responded Mansfield.

"Fracking, blowing up mobile homes, running my wife off the road, and buying property around town as a front— Up here, it's Pat Coruthers." Now Parker's ire was rising.

"Settle down, Parker. What about a mobile home?" Brooks asked.

"Sam and I went to visit the home of a missing local, and some sonovabitch blew it up—we were lucky to get out in time."

"Parker, I had no idea."

"You were right there, Brooks. You were watching the guy who I think did it."

"He never followed you. In fact, he headed south to Grand Rapids. The local reports I received were that it was a gas leak."

"Local reports?" Parker looked over at Johnson who was intently watching Moore's expressions.

"Yes. The Crawford County sheriff."

"Okay. What about the car chase?"

"I apologize ..." Brooks started but Johnson cut him off.

"Now, wait Moore. Brooks called that in to us, and we intervened."

"Yes, Parker." Brooks was going to finish. "I had his Escalade marked from a distance, and caught up as soon as I saw him all over my screen driving through the neighborhoods. I'm sorry Sam had to go through that. It was totally unexpected. By the way, the perp's name is Dimitri Anakova; and he's disappeared."

Parker sat back in his chair and looked at Tim Johnson. "Okay. Okay. What's this call about?"

"It's all gone quiet, Parker. No phones, texts, emails. Zilch. Nada. Nothing," Mansfield said. "We were wondering what you were seeing."

"I see Pat Coruthers from Grand Rapids Resources as a front for the super PAC Resources For All. I see the Governor of Michigan involved, along with some legislators, in fracking. I see my wife in danger because she's fighting the good fight." Parker was stern but steady in his delivery.

Tim Johnson was taking notes as fast as people were talking.

"But, I do have an idea." Parker smiled. "I've been working with our local billionaire, John Stanley, attempting to put a special project in place for him that would provide employment to hundreds in the middle part of the state, right where the fracking hailstorm is located."

"And?" John Brooks wondered aloud.

"Brooks, the river is a mess. Thursday night, I walked through snowpack and mud that had a chemical sheen to it. That was just before some gorilla tried to take me out."

"What?!" Johnson said.

"Forgot that one, boys. I went to scout the property of the man who is missing, Dorian Gray, and stumbled upon a nearby fracking site. Some guy came out of nowhere and began to play rough. I was rougher. Anyway, the local militia is suspicious of the fracking sites now that their oldest and most-trusted member is MIA. I'm pretty sure it was their commander who knocked me upside the head." Parker was anxious to finally get all the facts on the table.

"The idea Parker, the idea?" Mansfield asked.

"I have a team in Lansing that has secured Stanley's land for the project, and they're getting me an audience with the governor. I've set up a super PAC for John Stanley called Midwest Employment for All People, and delivered the first check to the National Republican Party in D.C. They're already running TV and radio spots for certain members of Congress who need assistance with their next election. I also have Stanley talking with Sir Edward Framingham for an invite to join Resources For All, so you can secure an insider they trust. You make sure no one shoots my ass, and I think we can prove once again that the Citizens United decision has taken things way too far."

"What do you need from us?" Mansfield asked. He and Brooks were leaning on the table looking at their speaker phone.

"I need you to come here and visit Stanley to set him up as your informant. Then, Supervisor Mansfield, I need your permission to press the Governor of Michigan. I need to come back into service, John."

Tim Johnson stopped writing and looked up, puzzled. John Brooks looked over at his supervisor, with a similar expression.

"Parker, you're outta line. That was a long time ago." Mansfield didn't hesitate in his answer. He was angry with Parker for revealing his previous employment with the NSA; he felt Brooks's pressing glare.

"John, I can do this. We can do this. I need to come back. I know it's been twenty years, but it's time." Parker was as surprised as anyone by his request.

"Parker, we'll talk later." Mansfield tried to smile at Brooks.

"No. Now. I know who was driving the Buick when Stefanie was killed. I know you ordered it. I know Stimson had my history when we met in D.C. Just let me get this done. I'm in it for Sam now. She needs me to be a hero." He paused and looked down at the table. Then he looked back at the speaker phone. "I need to be a hero again."

Tim Johnson looked like a statue. His gaping mouth and wide eyes couldn't hide his enormous surprise.

"Okay, goddamn it. Okay. Shit. Go after the governor. I'll get your credentials fired up again, but I'm warning you, Parker, this better work, because if it doesn't, it's my ass. Brooks is coming your way to meet with Stanley. And, Moore?"

"Yes, sir?" Parker could barely sit still.

"I've got a man deep. We'll take care of Resources For All. You take care of the cleanup."

"As long as you make my crucifixion a little less public this time. I don't mind staying deep on my turf, but give me a lifeline this time." Parker was smiling and looking at Johnson's stunned face.

"Deal. We'll talk later." Mansfield pushed a button to end the call. John Brooks was as frozen as Tim Johnson.

# TWENTY-SEVEN

"I KNEW IT! I KNEW IT SINCE OUR FIRST INTERVIEW when I was still a dick right outta uniform." Tim Johnson was following Parker up the stairs. "They killed your ex-wife and made it look like an accident because she was in this too. Jesus! I knew it. They wanted me to find her. They manipulated all of it."

"Look, Tim," Parker stopped, turned around, and looked down the steps at his out-of-breath friend. "You're mostly right. They did what they did because she was bought and paid for on the wrong payroll. I didn't know it until after she was dead. I suspected and found she had hacked into my phone, emails, and everything everywhere. She had help. The same people that continue to cause me, you, us problems. But, I'm still deep. I'm still quiet Parker Moore who writes poetry and consults around town."

They continued up the stairs.

"Does Sam know?" Johnson asked.

"No."

"Anyone know?"

Both men stopped as Parker turned to answer. "No."

They both continued walking the stairs.

"I knew it! I knew it." Johnson shook his head as he followed Parker through the door. "When do you head for Lansing?"

"As soon as I hear about a meeting, but I have a couple calls to make, and I want Sam back from her meeting in Frederic before I leave."

Parker put out his right hand to Johnson as they reached the front doors of the Public Safety Building. Johnson shook it and smiled. As Parker stepped outside, Johnson turned around, and mumbled to himself as he returned to his office.

† † †

Parker pulled out his phone as he walked east on Lake Street up the hill toward downtown.

"Senator."

"Moore. Is it time?"

"Almost. The check cleared and your committee's on board?"

"It did and they are. The GOP loves the idea and appreciates the TV time.

"Good. I'll call you, probably in the next couple days."

"Fine. We'll be ready. Tell John Stanley thanks ... this will be big, Parker." Senator Coolridge put his phone down on the table and returned to reading the *Wall Street Journal* in his favorite leather chair at the Capital Club in Washington, D.C.

† † †

"What the hell? All the shit that's gone down up there—now I know why!" John Brooks was pacing in Mansfield's office. "From the time we visited him in 2005, Todd thought there was more than we knew, but we just followed orders."

"And, it helped take down some very bad politicians and turn things around for us." Mansfield was still sitting at the table. He looked up and followed Brooks back and forth as he answered.

"Twenty years ago?" Brooks stopped pacing.

"It was a long-term strategy of NSA to have individuals throughout the United States we could rely on when we needed them. Parker did odd jobs here and there, but when the super PAC thing began we called in lots of folks. When those same people started dying, or being killed, we knew something was afoul. We got the big fishes and Washington cleaned out. Sad about the Supreme Court justice. Poor Agent Fletcher had a tough day."

"Now Dubai again?"

"Why not? Political money is legal and unlimited in the states. To think these groups that can control everything with money are going to be honest in their reporting—sheesh." Mansfield just shook his head. "A trillion-dollar group that has bought its way into the United States ... Sir

Edward might have been admonished by the Brits for what happened, but he's the most powerful oil mogul in the world. Number Ten Downing Street doesn't scare him, nor does MI6–he was an agent during the Cold War."

"So, why do we get involved if what they're doing is mostly legal?"

"It's not legal the way they do it, and it's our job to level the playing field." John Mansfield stood up and looked out the window. "You've got to get that flight to Pellston. The plane will be ready at Andrews, but first, sit down, John. Let's talk about Todd Ramsey."

# TWENTY-EIGHT

PARKER WAS LOOKING OUT THEIR BEDROOM WINDOW. He watched the lightning stab Lake Michigan. The distant sky flashed every few seconds; then forked lightning and the rumble of thunder coursed up the harbor, up the street, and into the house. Sam was not home yet. His jaw was tight. He could feel her absence; a tension as great as the storm outside. He'd tried all night to reach her, but to no avail. Her voicemail was the only answer. Waves of anxiety heightened the stress in each mandible. *It's not like her. It's like Stefanie all over again—but Sam wasn't Stefanie. There was something else. Danger. She should have been home from the meeting in Frederic hours ago. Two a.m. Jesus!* Parker decided to wait one more hour, and then he'd head out.

His phone rang. "Sam?!" he yelled into the phone.

"Parker! Parker! Oh, my god. I love you." She was out of breath.

"Sam, what happened? Where are you?" Parker was putting on his shoes and holding the phone between his shoulder and cheek. He set it down and put the speaker on.

"I'm at your mother's, and she's making me some tea. I'm safe."

"Are you alone?"

"No. The Crawford County deputies are with me—and your mom."

"I'll be right there." Parker was done with his shoes and rushed down the stairs. He wasn't running, but his protective instincts were in full gear. He was acting methodically.

"Okay. But please, I'm safe. Don't kill yourself." Sam was calm and sitting on one of the kitchen stools. The deputies were in two clusters talking and smoking, one inside the house and one out.

Parker was already in his truck and driving down the alley behind their home.

"Parker, really ..." Sam tried to laugh to alleviate her fear. "I'm okay."

"Be there in an hour."

"Your mother says don't rush. Thanks, honey."

Parker paid no attention to the mellowness of Sam's voice. She was not one to panic—why the police? It was supposed to have been a community meeting about fracking. Parker knew the Swamp could be a rough bar, but not for a town-hall meeting. His mind kept picturing the half mile that is Frederic. From the cemetery behind the militia headquarters where his father is buried, north to the last party store as Old US-27 runs straight toward Otsego Lake and Gaylord. In between were the gas station, the Frederic Inn, the post office, and the Swamp.

The importance of the Swamp to this community was not to be taken lightly. Years ago it burned down, only to have the townsfolk band together and rebuild it within two weeks. They even added a meeting room and more pool tables. The Swamp was Frederic and Frederic was the Swamp.

When Parker's dad said he wanted to be buried in a town that reminded him of the frontier gravel strips of Alaska, he found the perfect place in Frederic. If the Almighty himself picked up the entire half mile and put it outside of Cantwell on the road to Denali, the Alaskan government wouldn't blink.

Parker was in Mancelona and ready to turn left off of US-131. He picked up his phone. "Sam?"

"Yes?"

"Everything still okay?"

"Yes. The deputies are sitting at the table drinking coffee. I'm resting by the fireplace."

"What the hell happened?" Parker was headed toward Manistee Lake.

"Where are you?" Sam asked.

"Between Mancelona and Manistee Lake."

"I'll tell you when you get here. Cats inside?"

"Yes. The thunderstorm helped."

"Okay, Parker. You know Mike Ridley was playing tonight at the benefit."

"Yes."

"He's dead."

It was late and John Brooks was exhausted. The information he learned today had made his head spin; then flying to Pellston, grabbing the Buick, and driving to Frederic only to find a man outside the Swamp with a rifle was a bit much for one day. Brooks had driven up just as a robust figure was reloading his carbine and looking directly at the Swamp from across Old US-27. Brooks realized someone had already been shot since the crowd was stirring around inside, and the ambulance was pulling out of the fire garage just a couple hundred yards away. Some men with their weapons drawn ran out into the parking lot. *Stupid people*, he had thought.

Brooks immediately rammed the truck the man was standing behind with the Buick, which caused the man to drop his rifle, but by the time Brooks gathered himself and was out of his car, Glock in hand, the truck was speeding south on Old US-27. Brooks called the plate into 911 and relayed it to NSA. The return was instant: the 2012 Ford F-250 was registered to Harold Morris of Frederic Township. Hal Morris, Militia Commander. No lien on the truck which meant it was bought with cash. *Who the hell buys a fifty-thousand-dollar truck with cash in Frederic?* he wondered.

Brooks had watched the commotion that emanated from the Swamp from a distance. There were Crawford County sheriff cruisers everywhere, when suddenly two took off southbound on 27. He watched as the deputies found the weapon, and then he watched Sam Moore get into a patrol car with two more deputies. Once they headed west on CR-612, Brooks knew where they were going; so he left, driving south to his hotel room in Grayling, where he lay in bed and watched the movie *The Kingdom*. He thought about all the time he'd spent in the Middle East. It was always about the security of the oil–that is oil the U.S. bought and worked to get. Maybe fracking was the answer. In John Brooks's mind, no more Osama bin Ladens was a good thing; however, purchasing a political system for the world's wealthy was just as bad.

He finally dozed.

f f f

Parker parlayed his way through the mud and gravel of the dirt roads toward his mother's house on the Manistee River. He slowly pulled into the drive, only to have the deputies force him to stop. After a quick ID check, he was on the steps to the deck and into the house.

"I'm so glad you're here." Sam met him at the door. She began to cry softly. "Your mom went to bed."

Parker said nothing. He hugged his wife then led her over to the fireplace, sat her down, and said he'd be back after he talked with the deputies who were in the kitchen.

"What happened?" he asked the only sergeant on site, who he recognized from years past as the local patrol deputy.

"Your wife had the crowd whipped into a frenzy about fracking. Both pro and con groups started getting loud, so Van Der Knacht ended the meeting. He walked out with Hal Morris as his personal bodyguard, and about a half hour later all hell broke loose."

"What happened to Mike Ridley?" Parker looked back at Sam, who was staring at him.

"Looks like he just got in the way. The shots were aimed high. Like no one was supposed to have been hit. But when he walked offstage and in front of the window, well, that's when it all started. He's tall, and he's dead."

"Any idea who?"

"We got word about the truck and plate through an anonymous 911 call. It was Hal Morris. We found him at home sitting in his living room. We found the weapon across the street from the Swamp. Detectives will do the rest, since Morris had a mouthpiece in a suit with a checkbook in hand waiting for him. He'll make bail real quick."

"Anonymous?"

"Restricted call to be precise."

Sam walked over to the two men. She held Parker's left arm as they stood next to the kitchen counter.

"Thanks, Ted. I think we've got it from here." Parker looked down at Sam and smiled.

"You sure?"

"Yup. I think you found the bad guy."

"Okay. Call us if you need anything," said the deputy as he turned and left with his other officers.

Parker and Sam returned to the fireplace and sat on the loveseat. He thought about telling her she was safe and all would be well; instead he simply kissed her on the cheek as she rested against his chest. She was asleep in minutes.

*The masked man came late at night and stayed the entire next day. He made sure he talked with everyone, but spent most of his time at the wellhead closest to the private runway on the edge of the gas field. The residents wished him well, knowing they would never see him alive again. The man had surrendered to Allah, and found peace knowing in whatever world he found himself, it would be a purer life than this–even if heaven brought him hardship.*

*The only detail not discussed was the future of the well sites. That was in Allah's hands.*

# TWENTY-NINE

SUNDAY, APRIL 24

"SAM, I THINK IT'S ABOUT TIME YOU TOOK A BREAK. Mobile homes blowing up. Car chases. A shooting. I do believe someone is listening to you," Parker said as they sat in his mother's kitchen having a cup of coffee.

The Manistee River gurgled just outside the windows. The tag alders were coming into early buds and the tamarack needles were ready to make an appearance. The only birds were chickadees and some late juncos.

"But why? Fracking goes on in how many states? I'm glad someone is listening but now I'm curious. Why all the attention? Why now?" Sam was staring at the same scene.

"We'll find out, in due time. I still think Pat Coruthers is our man."

"Why? He could buy the world. Why chase someone off?"

Parker wasn't going into Sir Edward, the worldwide connection to a super PAC, and trillions of dollars in political money. For one, he understood the game these guys played, and it was all about ego and every dollar they could get. If someone got in the way of millions, and perhaps billions, of dollars being added to their coffers … suddenly he realized that Sir Edward might know about his past connection to the NSA. Well, of course he did! Thus, the interest in Sam being a part of the anti-fracking fabric. If she succeeds in stopping the newest fracking ground, what would happen in the other states? Add a new concept in employing people, and the need for fracking goes away–at least in Michigan. Parker couldn't tell Sam about the NSA, and he had to keep a level tone about the Stanley project in Frederic.

"I don't know. Right now we need to secure Stanley's idea for a clothing factory."

"They're ready," Sam said.

“Ready for what?” he asked, feeling his breathing change as he waited for her answer.

“Well, I sort of put a bug into their ears about it; versus fracking. Saving the water. You know.”

“Sam, that might be the best thing you’ve done.” Parker stood. “Let’s go for a walk.”

ť ť ť

The man walking around the neighborhood of estates in Kentwood just outside of Grand Rapids drew no special attention. There was a dog, a black trench coat, and expensive Johnston & Murphy’s. There was no one home in the house he walked in front of twice.

He watched.

Quietly.

ť ť ť

Pat Coruthers wasn’t happy about the response he received from his attorney about the incident at Chandler’s the other night, but there was nothing he could do about it. Sir Edward was emphatic about Coruthers staying low and going about the business of expanding test sites into the billions of dollars in natural gas that simmered far below the surface of the Great Lakes. He decided to take his wife on a shopping trip to downtown Petoskey, where he could visit his business properties and enjoy his wife’s company.

ť ť ť

“Where are we going, Parker? This is muck, and, um, muck.” Sam was taking big steps in scattered snowpack and troughs of mud.

The property Parker’s father purchased in 1980 had acres of black spruce that had somehow missed the loggers’ blades and the statewide fires in the early 1900s. They passed the property-survey marker and continued into the swamps and tamarack. It was Parker’s place of solitude along the river.

“Just wanna get away, Sam. A lot’s hatching around us. I can feel it. Time to find the rhythm of the woods." Parker trudged on, but his longer legs made navigating the cool tussock path easier.

"Can't we just find a meadow?" Sam had to watch every step as she tried to keep up.

After a few hundred feet, they were out of the damp tussocks and into a jack pine forest heading toward the gas line and Goose Creek Road. Parker wanted to get to the clear stream of Goose Creek and watch the early trout boiling in the shallow water. Sam hit the dry land and walked faster, passing Parker who was looking around with every step.

"Keep your nose up, Sam. Early bears. See?" He pointed to some logs ripped apart for ants and termites.

As Sam took another step, she stopped and gasped. "Parker!"

He ran a few steps ahead of her and looked down.

John Brooks was having breakfast at the hotel in Grayling while he read the encrypted emails from headquarters on his phone. The email about the rifle involved in the shooting at the Swamp said:

*Gun was registered to Dorian Gray of Frederic Township. Whereabouts unknown. Home destroyed in a natural gas explosion.*

"Bullshit," he said to himself as he remembered Parker's comments.

Another email was about Commander Hal Morris of the militia being released to a lawyer.

Using his cover as a land surveyor, Brooks was to drive to Harbor Springs for the day and work on some FEMA questions concerning flood plains near the local rivers—the issue Parker's mother had challenged him about. Brooks knew it was a controversial subject locally, but it helped protect his cover. He'd also meet with Parker Moore and John Stanley.

Standing outside the Lake Affect store on Howard Street, Pat Coruthers checked his phone while his wife shopped inside. He had missed a call from ADT. Apparently the alarm system in his home had gone off; he dialed the phone number.

"ADT."

"This is Pat Coruthers of 459 Longbark Way in Kentwood. I missed a call."

"Certainly, Mr. Coruthers. Could you hold a moment?"

He said nothing, and turned away from the front store window and looked up the street.

"Could you give us your password, sir?"

"JDRockefeller3."

"Very well, sir. Your alarm was triggered this morning, but I want to assure you, we had the police and our agents out there immediately, and all was secure. We reset the system from this office."

Since there were false alarms from various causes that occurred even when he was in the house, Coruthers shrugged his shoulders and thought nothing of it. "Okay. Keep me posted, please, if anything else happens."

"Yes, sir. Most assuredly. Thank you, Mr. Coruthers," the nervous voice responded.

Coruthers placed his phone in his pocket and walked into Lake Effect.

† † †

"I wonder who it is," Sam said with her right hand covering her nose and mouth.

The body and clothing were in tatters. Both arms and legs were separated, with the muscle and skin mostly gone from the legs. The face was leathered and shrunken. Parker looked at it and thought instantly of a cadaver in undergrad anatomy. He bent down and rested his knee beside the corpse careful not to touch anything. The ground around the body was clawed and coyote and bear scat littered the area. He looked up and around. This was a rarely visited part of Goose Creek, well off the beaten path and only known by a few. Only game paths traversed the area.

Parker knew who it was. "Sam. Meet Dorian Gray. Or should I say his portrait. Looks like he finally met the devil. "

# THIRTY

HANNAH WAS MAKING JOHN STANLEY'S MARTINI, POURing the Laphroaig for Parker Moore, and a club soda for a new face. She was the only other person in the bar.

"So, John, meet John," Parker began as they sat at a high booth at the Bar Harbor bar. "Sorry I'm late. Sam and I ran into an old friend we had to make some arrangements for."

"Mr. Stanley." John Brooks nodded at the gentleman across from him.

"Mr. Brooks." John Stanley returned the greeting. He began to cough.

"You alright, John?" Parker asked concerned as he placed his left hand on Stanley's back.

"I'm fine. Just old." Stanley's cancer was progressing rapidly. He'd let no one know. "So, what is it you do, Mr. Brooks?"

"Well, actually it's Agent Brooks. He's with the NSA," Parker said as he stared at John Brooks, looking for an expression change. It didn't happen.

"Then, this must be about your plan with Sir Edward?" Stanley asked as he looked at Parker.

"Yes. Yes it is."

"Mr. Brooks …" Stanley paused as Hannah brought over their drinks.

"Anything else?" she asked.

"We're fine, Hannah. Some privacy, please," Stanley said as he shook her hand and passed along five one-hundred-dollar bills.

Hannah smiled and walked over to the front door. She locked it and walked into the back.

"Now, Mr. Brooks. I have contacted Sir Edward. He is awaiting a meeting."

Parker and Brooks looked at each other. Brooks knew nothing of Parker's plan. He waited.

"Actually, I wanted to ask if you'd be willing to wear a wire, John," Parker said.

"To the meeting?" John Stanley sipped his Hendricks martini. There were no olives.

"Yes."

"Okay. Why?" Stanley asked.

"We need to have an insider in a group of billionaires who meet in Dubai. They own the oil and gas markets and in turn use the money to purchase political influence," John Brooks said as he quickly caught on. He was leaning toward John Stanley and compassionate in his response.

"In the long run, John, it will help us with your factory in Frederic."

"How?"

"This super PAC, Resources For All, has influence in that area," Parker answered.

"A super PAC? I thought it was an oil and gas company? GRR? Is that the same thing you started for me, Parker?" Stanley asked.

"Kind of. Except we don't wish to rule the world. But, John, honestly, yes. You're buying influence," Parker said chagrined.

"It's both. In this case, the lines have become blurred. People have died over this one," Brooks said. "And the influence is through this group that meets in Dubai."

"As I said, he's waiting. Where shall I tell him to meet?" Stanley seemed satisfied with the answers.

Parker looked at Brooks and thought momentarily. "Turkmenistan," Parker said.

"Turkmenistan," Brooks reiterated looking at Parker then Stanley.

"Turkmenistan," John Stanley repeated as he toasted his martini toward the two.

† † †

"So, Mr. Mansfield, you've reconnected with someone you used in the past and now we find out it's the same person we also used in the past?" said the Chair of the Super PAC. They were sitting at the round conference table in the room below NSA headquarters.

"That's, um, correct, ma'am," Mansfield said as he cleared his throat. "We, ah, needed to make the connection for the purpose of our goal," he stuttered.

"Very well." She looked around the table at the five other members. "We don't have a problem with that. Is the purpose a continuation of our pursuit of the Dubai obstacle?"

"Yes. And we now have a pretty good handle where their money has been going," Mansfield responded in a more comfortable tone.

"Which is?" the Attorney General asked.

"Local: states, cities, and townships."

"For?" the AG probed.

"Fracking. They continue to utilize their political capital to grow their wealth and in turn fund their super PAC with more capital than anyone else can match. In fact, as the United States becomes more energy independent, this group becomes more powerful." Mansfield was becoming passionate in his tone.

"We have documented proof of this?" asked another member of the group.

"Let us say, we have circumstantial evidence, but we are close to hard data. We have several staff looking in new places for accounts and chatter," John Mansfield continued with a confident voice. "The EPA studies that will be published in 2014 may shed some damaging light on the fracking industry. In fact, a recent find from Alberta exhibited a water table contaminated with benzene, toluene, ethylbenzene, and xylene, also known as BTEX. Highly carcinogenic. The chemical mix made it into drinking water."

"So?" the chair asked.

"We believe Resources For All will make adjustments to maximize their wealth prior to the release of the EPA findings. We also have California coming online as a battleground state in the fracking debate. The *LA Times* has continued to report fracking of wells under people's property without their knowledge. The same thing we now have in Michigan. The threat to the Great Lakes is immense, and we also believe this group knows more about what's under the Great Lakes than we do."

"This hasn't turned into some witch hunt for something that could be beneficial to the country, has it, Mr. Mansfield?" asked Mr. Roberts, a member with close ties to the oil and gas industry. He was leaning across the table with both hands perched on the desk.

"Sir, I assure you, our purpose is not about fracking per se; however, the money connected to the fracking has become a threat to our sovereign democracy. Our mission is to protect the United States from all threats to that sovereignty. I may be describing the fracking industry, but I also must comment on the threats and objective knowledge we have. If that is against an economic belief you or this group has that is not for me to decide."

"Your job, Director Mansfield, is to do what we tell you to do," the gentleman from Texas almost came out of his chair when he spoke.

Mansfield didn't blink.

"Gentlemen. Mr. Roberts. I understand your connection to this issue and the passion you may have, but Mr. Mansfield is only doing what we've asked. The rest of us believe the threat to be real. Do you object?" The Chairperson maintained her calm as she looked at each member, ending with Mr. Roberts.

"No. I'm sorry. Perhaps I should recuse myself of this."

"That's not possible. You are a vetted member of this organization. If you disagree, we simply move on with majority opinion. If you disagree, you are held to an oath to maintain the secrecy of our decisions."

"Mr. Mansfield," Mr. Roberts began. "I am sorry. The industry you describe was near and dear to my heart. But, I am out of it now and only offer consultation. Please understand that fifty years is hard to bury, but I do understand the difficulty you are in." He turned to the Chair, "Madame, I assure you, I am fully onboard. Continue." He sat back in his chair and took a deep breath.

"Thank you. We tread difficult waters here. Some of what is going on is legal under the Supreme Court decision we must live with. Some of it is not." Chairman Rialto turned her gaze back to Mansfield. "John, I ask you to make whatever field decisions you must to protect our sovereignty from this clear and present danger. I will promise a meeting with the President and a plan for connected public policy, and press to make sure that what may happen can be fully explained. Is that clear yet vague enough for you to work?"

"Yes, ma'am." John Mansfield said, smiling as he stood and shook hands with Mr. Roberts.

Roberts stood, smiled, and nodded his head.

"Gentlemen. Until next time." Rialto stood and looked at the members before her. She was not going to redress her decision. Everyone understood and quietly exited the room.

John Mansfield was last to leave. He found a quiet alcove and punched a number into his cell phone. The contact in Azerbaijan was informed of the decision. He then placed a call to John Brooks.

"John, we're a go," he said.

“Okay. We’re headed to Lansing. Stanley’s waiting for our go-ahead,” Brooks answered.

“I’ll be in touch.” Mansfield ended the call. He ran his right hand through his hair and looked down at the floor with a deep sigh.

*The West wanted fossil fuels for energy, but didn't want the burden of destroying property, land, and the environment in their backyard to get it. Out of sight, out of mind was easy while they drove their BMWs and Land Rovers from church, to soccer games, and shopping malls. Now prospectors had developed a new technology to obtain that energy while not appearing so destructive to the environment—or so they thought. The men in the gas and oilfields of Turkmenistan didn't have the luxuries of the West—promises, yes; luxuries, no. And the land in the Middle East was poisoned.*

*The day will come when land in the West is poisoned in the name of profit and capitalism. Yes. The day will come.*

# THIRTY-ONE

**MONDAY, APRIL 25**

PARKER WAS GETTING OUT OF THE SHOWER AS SAM FINished putting on her makeup. Just as he put his towel on the hook and grabbed his robe, the phone rang. He ran to the bedroom, thinking it was John Brooks with news about their trip to Lansing, but as he looked at the number he saw it was Kathi.

"Parker? He was here," she said sounding calm but there was a concerned temper to her voice.

"Coruthers?" Parker answered.

"Yes. He did exactly what you said. He said there was a mistake in the lease and he must ask for several hundred dollars more a month. I told him just what you said to."

"And?"

"He looked surprised and he said he'd sell the store. You sure your friend can help?"

"It's done, Kathi. Keep the dream alive. Your store is fine." Parker heard his phone beep in his ear and looked at the number. It was Brooks. "Kathi, I have to go. We'll catch up later." He switched calls. "John. Ready?"

"I am. Pick me up on the way. I'll be at the truck stop on 4 Mile Road."

"Got it." Parker put down his phone and walked into his dressing room. Sam passed him in the hallway. The cats started racing downstairs but stopped; they were waiting for someone to get them breakfast.

"Going out?" she asked Parker as she slapped him on the butt. "Feed the cats on your way."

"Lansing. Have a visit with the gov. And, yes, come on, Kali. Come on, Keeper." Both cats bolted by him down the stairs, but Parker stayed upstairs and walked over to Sam.

"Lance and Rance?" she said laughing as she walked into her closet.

"Yes. The boys got me in."

"Will you be home tonight?" Sam asked as she walked into the hall buttoning her white blouse.

"Not sure. I'll try. Plans?"

"Yes." She reached up and grabbed Parker around the neck and kissed him. "Don't wear yourself out." She let him go and whistled Billy Joel's "Always a Woman to Me" as she walked back into her closet.

Parker could only smile and finish tying his tie.

"Sam, I'm outta here. Love you." He walked down the stairs and his affect turned serious. "It's your turn, gov," he said as he opened a can of cat food.

ƒ ƒ ƒ

The masked man in Azerbaijan made his way over to the private jet. He boarded and awaited his trip to Ashgabat, the capitol of Turkmenistan, and from there a long truck ride to Serhetabat. The companions he'd nurtured for months would be waiting.

ƒ ƒ ƒ

The Coruthers's house in Grand Rapids was ready for their return. After clearing security, the man sat in the bar at the Gerald R. Ford International Airport. He asked for a glass of vodka. No ice.

ƒ ƒ ƒ

Parker drove south on U.S.-131 to M-32 and then south on I-75. He thought of the task before him. Assumptions that the Governor of Michigan and local legislators were the new victims of money from a super PAC from afar were just that–assumptions. He would look the governor in the eyes and make it known all was about to be uncovered. All was about to become public. Unless he was willing to stop the allowance of fracking in the Great Lake State and work toward other means of revenue including green manufacturing that would employ thousands. The first of these factories would be in Frederic Township, a prize for his legislators, who would be reeling from the change, yet relieved to know their reputations would be protected; and the Federal government would give them a pass. To add to the prize, money would arrive from Congress to assist John Stanley with his legacy. Parker smiled at his plan, but worried about some unknown details.

Sir Edward was one of the richest men in the world and he wanted the Great Lakes. His money solved everything. How would his part end? Parker felt a chill as he drove up the exit ramp onto 4 Mile Road south of Grayling. John Brooks was dressed in a suit and waiting near the front door of the gas station and convenience store.

"Hey, Parker," Brooks said as he climbed into Parker's truck. "Right on time."

"You ready for this?"

Brooks shut the door and buckled his seatbelt. "No. I'm ready to ask you what the hell you've been doing schlepping around as a regular civilian while we watched your ass and made sure you stayed safe. How did you pull that off?"

Parker put the truck into gear and looked over at his companion, trying not to smile. "Sorry, John," he said seriously. "But that's classified. If I told you, I'd have to kill you." He spun the tires as he drove off the dirt onto the pavement.

# THIRTY-TWO

TONY BENNETT'S RENDITION OF THE OLD HAROLD ARLEN tune "I've Got the World on a String" was playing on the CD as the two men made their way south on U.S.-127 toward Lansing. They'd just passed the first exit for Clare when Parker's phone vibrated.

"Moore," he answered.

"Parker, you know that shooting in Frederic, where Mike Ridley was killed?" Tim Johnson was calling from his office.

"Yeah?"

"They found a complete confession written out."

"By?"

"Not sure. Locals said it's from the man they found in the driver's seat of his new Ford F-250 parked back in Upper Manistee River Campground. Oh, and he had a bullet hole in his head."

"Commander of the Militia."

"How'd you know?"

"Hunch."

"He wasn't alone. There were two other victims with him. Same holes; same gun. One was a missing lawyer they've been looking for. His Range Rover was found near Grand Rapids a while back—clean as a whistle. Third guy they think was a professional assassin from Chicago."

Parker looked at Brooks. "You been looking for a Range Rover, by any chance?"

Brooks nodded. *Dimitri Anakova* he thought.

"Thanks, Tim. Brooks is with me. By the look on his face, I suspect this wraps a few things up."

"One more thing," Johnson brought his feet off his desk and grabbed a piece of paper. "There was a message with the bodies not in Hal Morris's handwriting."

"Yeah?"

"Oo-dach-I," Johnson said slowly in his best attempt at Russian "Good luck."

"Shit. You are a spook. That was written in Russian."

"You've met him," Parker said.

"Anakova. The guy who chased Sam down?" Johnson said.

"The same."

"Guess he's still out there, and that dead lawyer was in my office to rescue him." Johnson was standing and looking out at the empty marina. His stomach tightened. "I'll put someone in the house with Sam."

"Thanks, Tim, but I think your man isn't a worry anymore. I'll call you after we leave Lansing."

"Just the same, I'll have someone with her. See ya, Parker." Johnson hung up the phone and instinctively placed his right hand on his holstered weapon. He continued gazing outside, hoping Parker was right.

"What gives?" Brooks asked as they approached Mount Pleasant.

"Your man, Anakova, still seems to be spookier than you—and me. They found Commander Morris shot in his truck, and two other guys from your Range Rover with him—a lawyer and a hit man from Chicago. MOs were the same."

Brooks didn't say anything. He felt a sense of failure grab at him. His mark wasn't gone and now three dead bodies. He was familiar with death, had faced death, and killed, but his conscience was still that of a good guy, and the fact that he had a conscience in this business always made it difficult. He stared out the window at the passing scenery. The early spring green and freshly planted fields provided a less grim view.

"John, there was also a note in Russian. It said *good luck*. I think he's not our problem anymore."

Brooks looked at Parker. Face taut. Still silent.

"I think he's Coruthers's worst nightmare," Parker said as he glanced at Brooks and then returned to watching the freeway ahead of him.

Suddenly a smile came over John's sullen face, and he averted his gaze from the scenery to his hands as he rubbed them slowly in his lap. He looked up at Parker. "I guess when you try to kill someone and they don't like it, they carry a grudge."

"And I think Dimitri Anakova is the last person you'd want holding a grudge against you," Parker replied.

"So, Parker … how and why?" Brooks seemed re-energized since realizing it wasn't an error on his part that caused the deaths.

"How and why what?" Parker was sure he knew what Brooks wanted to know, but needed to rope-a-dope for a moment.

"The NSA. Us and what we allowed to happen to you."

"I always wanted to be the hero, John. I wasn't exactly innocent, but when you grow up feeling alone in a cold family, you spend the rest of your life trying to connect. Trying to make sure everyone likes you. That they find value in you."

"So the abuse wasn't just from your ex?" Brooks was acting the therapist and liked it. Everyone in the NSA who worked in the field constantly went through debriefings with therapists and professional counselors to maintain some kind of humanness.

"No." Parker smiled a half smile. His eyes welled up–always did. "I'm the one who has to take responsibility for putting myself in abusive situations. Just a pattern of doing things thinking they were right but instead they led to my own detriment."

"But your cover. It was so convincing."

"It was easy. My life was a cover. Now it's not, and I have Sam to thank for that. By the way, I know you folks eliminated Stefanie—who did it?"

"An asset from Ann Arbor. One of our best. She used the Buick I was driving a few days ago," Brooks said sheepishly. "You know about Stefanie being wired in to all of your information, but did you know she was implicated with the Dubai group? Seems they approached her with enough money, and she didn't hesitate. Once Sir Edward's security staff found out you had overheard their conversation in Juneau, they were convinced you would be their demise. I guess they were right." Brooks took a moment before he finished. "And, now that people are acting the fool around Sam, you want peace, but … ?"

"My way now. Mansfield could sense that. He knew." Parker continued nonchalantly, "Ann Arbor, eh?"

The truck had passed Mount Pleasant and they were rounding the curve east toward a small stretch of old highway between Ithaca and St. Johns.

"How are your kids?" Brooks took a sip of water from his water bottle.

"Great. They're off and running and perfect. Each generation makes the next generation better, John. That's the goal." Parker felt proud anytime he was able to talk of his children—a sincere gratitude always in the background.

"Cool. I always wanted kids, but still can't find the right woman." He put his water bottle back in the console and smiled as he looked out the side window. "Maybe it's time for a desk."

"Tried it. Didn't like it," Parker said.

"No, really. I think this might be it. This is young people's work and I'm getting long in the tooth."

"At thirty-two? I would think that's prime."

"Nope. Anymore, the technology alone changes faster than your underwear." Brooks shifted his weight in his seat and held up his iPhone4.

Parker leaned over toward Brooks, and in his best Groucho Marx replied, "You've never seen my underwear."

He switched the CD player to Miles Davis playing "Kind of Blue."

# THIRTY-THREE

"SIR EDWARD, JOHN STANLEY HERE. I THOUGHT THIS should be a personal phone call and not between intermediaries." Stanley was standing in the living room of his home on Harbor Point. Lake Michigan was a midnight blue with random whitecaps strewn about from a growing westerly wind.

"Ah, right. John. How gracious. Have you given my proposition continued thought?" Sir Edward replied. He was at his home in St. John's Woods in the City of Westminster, northwest of London, attending to his empty mansion. As a widower with no children, he amassed a fortune with no place to put it; so instead he manipulated the world as his own. Empathy was a learned virtue and any he had disappeared long ago with his time in Her Majesty's Secret Service. MI6 taught him how shallow life is. The only way to survive his world was no empathy or sympathy—it was only for show.

"Yes, Sir Edward. I have. I would like to discuss the entry by also viewing some land you frequent in Turkmenistan."

"Really? You keep track of things as you should. Why there?"

"I believe—" Stanley hesitated as he adlibbed from the rehearsed script he and Parker had reviewed, although he knew he had the Brit hooked. "I believe," he continued, "that has become one of your more lucrative plots, and if I'm going to assist you in North America, where I know you're already entrenched, I'd like to see something a little more challenging. See how you do in the outback, as it were."

"Wonderful. I appreciate your aplomb. When can we do this? I can have you meet Nazar." Sir Edward Framingham was surprised, elated, and suspicious all at the same time. He was already using his other hand to punch in Evgeny's number on the secure phone sitting on the bureau in front of him.

† † †

"We're getting the number, sir. He took the bait," said the voice over the speaker phone in his office.

"Great. Keep tabs on it and keep me posted." John Mansfield was relieved.

At last, a break. All had been silent until they set up the necessary measures around Sir Edward's estates, including drone flyovers. Mansfield typed a text into his phone.

**We have a positive contact between our parties. Good luck on your end.**

† † †

John Brooks received the text as he was walking into the Michigan State Capitol with Parker. Rance and Lance Hennessey were already with the governor in his private office.

"We're a go, Parker," Brooks said as he walked toward security on the ground-floor entry for guests.

Parker stopped and turned around to face Brooks. He needed to add some levity to what could be a difficult meeting. He also felt some angst being in a building with lots of history for him; not all good.

"How many Johns do we have on our side?" Parker said smiling at Brooks.

"Shut the fuck up, Moore, and move your ass. You gotta job to do." Brooks was laughing as he whispered and pushed Parker toward the security checkpoint and the Michigan State Police officer who had become curious about the pair.

"Gentlemen," the officer said as he watched the men carefully. He held his right hand over his weapon as a good measure.

"Don't worry, officer. We're the good guys," Parker said as he and Brooks placed their keys, wallets, and phones in a bowl on a conveyer running through the side of the scanner as they walked through the people side of the machine.

Parker had thought about having John pull out his NSA ID but that would have led to speculation and gossip by the officer. The two made their way up the grand staircase to the second floor and the governor's office. Once inside, the secretary and the governor's assistant led them into the governor's private chamber, where Rance, Lance, and Governor Sheldon were sitting around a conference table.

"Parker Moore, meet Governor Sheldon. And, I don't believe we've met." Rance walked around the table to Brooks and held out his right hand.

"Joseph Granger. How do you do?" Brooks continued his cover.

"Mr. Moore, it's a pleasure. I've heard a lot about you," Governor Sheldon said as he shook Parker's hand and directed him around the table with his left. The governor then shook hands with Brooks and pointed to the same side of the table where he sent Parker. "Can we get you something to drink? Coffee for me," he noted.

"Me too. Black," Parker said.

The governor's assistant looked at Brooks. "Black, thank you," he said, sitting down next to Parker.

The assistant left and Governor Sheldon returned to his seat. "To what do I owe this pleasure?"

"Well, actually, I was wondering if we could have a moment alone with you, sir. If that's okay with the Hennessey two?" Parker smiled and sat with his hands folded on the table.

"Rance and I have no objection. Governor?" Lance was already standing.

"Sure. Why not? I'll see you boys momentarily."

The Office of the Governor had recently been remodeled and had recaptured the essence of the Feige Brothers in Saginaw who originally furnished the office. The dark, walnut accents of the room were actually a paint process over pine and other cheaper woods; however, the ornate décor was a pleasure for a romantic like Parker Moore. He felt in his element. The angst was gone, the Hennessey brothers were gone, and the door shut. Parker looked at Brooks and began immediately.

"Your honor, this is actually John Brooks from the National Security Agency." Brooks showed his ID and federal badge. "We're here to present a proposal to you, and in all honesty, Governor, there's really no choice. I do apologize for the form of entry, but any other way would have drawn suspicion."

"So, this is not about John Stanley's project?" The governor looked cool and calm.

"Yes, but that's only part of it. We believe you've been—" Parker stopped mid-sentence. "No, we know you've been in contact with Sir

Edward Framingham." Parker stopped to watch for a reaction. He got it.

Governor Sheldon instantly stood up and walked over to his desk, as if he was in a 1930's movie. The dramatic effect was pronounced. He slowly turned back toward the two men at the table. "Yes." The governor was no fool. This was the NSA, and they were there for a reason. "What can I tell you?"

"For one thing, sir, please come sit. We'll make this as painless as possible. If all goes as planned, we can make you look like a hero to all sides concerned and take your legislature with you." Parker was doing all the talking. John Brooks was only there for the intimidation factor.

"Very well," the governor made his way back to the table.

There was a knock at the door. The assistant opened the heavy wood doors and stood, awaiting the gesture from the governor before bringing in the coffee service. He served coffee from the carafe to all three men. The governor used a little cream and sugar.

"Thank you, Norris. That will be all. Could you make sure we're not disturbed?" The governor began to sip his coffee as the assistant exited and closed the doors. "Now, where were we?"

"Now that the cat's out of the bag, what is Sir Edward holding over your head?" Parker sat back with his coffee cup cradled in both hands, and he wondered what the governor would have said had he known Parker was bluffing with an assumption.

"He's been using money from a super PAC, legally mind you, to stack the legislature and create a loud voice for oil and gas, especially fracking, and it's worked wonderfully well. We have become twelfth in the country as a producer state and, as you know, the U.S. is now ready to export more energy than we import. A rather quick turnaround, wouldn't you say?"

"Sir Edward's super PAC has done this all over the country – the world over, for that matter. We know we have to accept some of this expansion; however, in Michigan, it is a tenacious battle because of our fresh water," Parker interrupted.

"That's what he has on me! He, they, whoever, wants the gas, but mostly the water. He knows something we don't. He provided me a private retirement residence in the Caribbean. Bought and paid for."

"But you're a well-known millionaire. You could have done that on your own." Parker came forward in his chair, setting the coffee cup on the table.

"Yes, but he did it without my asking and threatened to go public. He has produced documents to make it look like it's a done deal with my acceptance. There is an island I now own, much to my chagrin." The governor's posture and face relaxed the more he talked. "I suppose I could take him on, but it would get ugly."

"Well, we're here to help. Now, we know Grand Rapids Resources has been a front for the super PAC. Are you familiar with them?" Parker was glancing at Brooks as he talked to the governor.

"Yes, I have. They're the company that holds almost all of the leases, well, now all, in the State of Michigan." The governor's interest was now peaked, since he hated dealing with Coruthers. "I never trusted that guy."

"Coruthers?" Brooks suddenly entered the conversation.

"Pat Coruthers, yes." The governor leaned over the table slightly and looked at both men facing him. "Please, don't take this the wrong way if you're friends of his, but I find him offensive."

"A tool, I would say," Parker shared. Brooks nodded and smiled. "You're going to hold a press conference and highlight a new legislative initiative against the future expansion of fracking, and you're going to announce John Stanley's initiative of a green textile factory in Frederic, employing hundreds. You'll also be able to announce future sites for other factories fostered by Stanley in each depressed area of the state, and that the United States Congress is passing legislation for assistance to your endeavors."

The governor was genuinely impressed. He sat back and rested his hands on the arms of his chair. "This has all been worked out? What about Sir Edward?" he asked.

"Leave Sir Edward to us, sir," said Brooks.

"Yes, Governor, this has all been set up," Parker added. "But, I do have one favor."

ǂ ǂ ǂ

An hour later, Parker and Brooks walked out of the governor's private office. Rance was the first to greet them. "What the hell was that all about?" he asked.

"Buy us a drink, and I can fill you in," Parker said as he opened the outer doors into the hallway for the group.

"Buy you a drink? Don't you think you should be buying?" Lance replied.

"Nope. Got lots more business for you two, and it will be quite the feather in your cap."

They made their way down the grand stairs. Parker glanced over to a familiar Senate hearing room where the intervention several years ago continued to rain from his synapses. The Senator that could have been saved but chose not to–his political life was more important than his own. Parker was glad he chose differently for himself.

"Parker, you are a mystery." Rance shook his head as the group closed in on the same security checkpoint they entered through.

After they exited the Capitol grounds and were walking toward East Michigan Avenue, Lance said, "I suppose it's going to be the most expensive scotch they have."

"You bettcha! Where did I hear that before?" Parker looked at Brooks and smiled.

The governor sat back in his chair, feeling the release of a heavy burden; yet, in disbelief of the political wrangling. Had he just been rescued from political death? Had he just become another pawn in the anti-fracking caper or the anti-super PAC movement? In any case, he was relieved that all would be positive in the end.

He pushed the intercom button on his phone. "Norris, get me John Stanley."

Sam walked out of her office. As she neared her car, two uniformed Petoskey public safety officers greeted her. At first, she was startled; then she was afraid of what they were going to tell her. Parker hadn't called all day. *What the hell did he do now?* She primed herself for the worst-case scenario.

"Mrs. Moore?" The older officer approached her first.

"Yes? Is there something wrong?" Sam stopped and waited for the verbal detonation.

"Chief, er, Director Johnson, would like us to accompany you home and stay with you until he arrives. There's no alarm, Mrs. Moore. Just precautions; he'll explain."

The officer opened her car door for her as the younger officer watched all around them. "Um, sure," Sam said, not knowing whether to be alarmed or relieved.

She drove out of the parking lot with one police SUV in the lead and another behind her. As she drove up to the next intersection, another police SUV turned in front of her. The four vehicles made their way to Sam's back alley and garage. One SUV pulled around front and the other two up the driveway after Sam pulled her car into the garage.

She walked to the back door. Before she could open it, the older officer stopped her, drew his Glock, and went in first. Now she was alarmed. The second officer waited with her. The other officers entered the front door at the same time. Her instinct was to be quiet and let the professionals handle it, but it was hard not to start asking questions.

Three officers checked the house as Sam quickly opened the back screen door, startling the young officer guarding her; they remained in the kitchen while the others searched the house.

"Clear," yelled one.

"Clear," said another.

"Clear," said the last.

"Now, can someone please tell me what the hell's going on?" Sam could be silent no longer. She put her purse on the counter and waited for an answer.

"Director Johnson is …"

The older officer was interrupted as Tim Johnson walked in the back door. "Hey, Sam. All good, boys?" He was in full uniform today.

"Yes, sir," the youngest answered quickly.

"Good. Thanks. You can all head out. Stay a few minutes in your vehicles though until I contact you." He turned to Sam. "It's about Dimitri Anakova. The man who chased you around the neighborhood. Turns out he might not have met his demise."

Suddenly Sam was relieved knowing the house was surrounded by police. In her best show of no fear, she looked calmly at Johnson. "You think he might be around here?"

"We're not sure. I talked with Parker earlier, and he didn't think it was a worry, but this guy is a really bad guy. I was the one who didn't want to take any more chances. Hell, I spend as much time on the job in this house anyway; so why not another visit?" Johnson was smiling as he tried to melt the tension. He really did not want to tangle with a former Russian GRU agent. "This is Petoskey, after all," he said finishing his thoughts out loud.

"What about Petoskey?" Sam was confused.

"Nothing. Have you heard from Parker?"

"No."

"Me neither."

"Surprised?"

"No."

"Money that his phone's off?"

"Twenty it's not," bet Johnson.

Sam put her phone on speaker and dialed. It went directly to Parker's voicemail. Johnson reached for his wallet and began to pull out a twenty dollar bill.

"Save it, Tim. How's about you buy at Roast & Toast?"

"Deal. But that's a lotta coffee."

"I'll order a really expensive latte fru-fru drink." Sam laughed as they made their way to the front door.

† † †

Pat Coruthers parked the car. They had just returned from their mini vacation up north. While his wife and son rummaged around in the Escalade for their phones, leftover drinks, and anything else they wanted to carry inside the house on the first trip, Pat was anxious to get inside.

He thought he got a whiff of natural gas as he approached the front door, but realized the wind was coming from behind and the smell was probably from neighboring grounds. He opened the door and pushed his code into the alarm pad just inside the foyer.

After the explosion, his wife and son looked up from behind the Escalade, where they'd been thrown ten feet back. The size of the large SUV saved them. There was nothing left of the front part of the house.

The son would report a jet flying overhead just as he and his mother were able to stand. The noise of the jet was strangely noticeable during the quiet aftermath of the blast.

# THIRTY-FOUR

THE CREW OF WELLHEAD NUMBER 120 OUTSIDE OF SERhetabat gathered for a meeting with the crews from the closet six or seven wellheads. The men were discussing the strike they planned to implement over the next two days. The masked man who began visiting months ago had suggested a group effort of peacefully sitting down and refusing to work. Violence would only beget violence, he preached; yet the men felt a coldness about him that reminded them of other Taliban that had attempted to woo them into Jihad.

Soon there would be a private jet that would park on the runway at the nearby airstrip. A caravan of white SUVs would drive by the striking workers and the idle worksites. The masked man assured the men that the owners of the fields would take notice. Only one day of the strike would be necessary.

Most of the men thought more would be necessary, but the strike was a first step to make the infidels take notice. None of the men were willing to sacrifice themselves in the name of Jihad. Their families were too important.

On the return from Lansing, John and Parker took turns driving. Both were tired and the days ahead would be busy. The traffic was almost non-existent, and the warm air allowed them to drive with the windows down. The breeze felt good and it helped both stay awake. The Doobie Brothers played loudly on the stereo, which took their minds off the next step. As they approached the M-32 exit in Gaylord off I-75, Parker's phone rang. He was surprised it was on. It was John Stanley.

Parker wasn't sure why he'd be calling so late; however, you didn't ignore a call from John Stanley.

"Hello, John," Parker said. Brooks was driving and singing along to "China Road."

"Moore. I wanted to tell you that Sir Edward is on board. He wants me to meet him at Heathrow and then travel with him to Turkmenistan on his private jet. I guess he will have some of his colleagues along." Stanley was formal and businesslike.

"That's great, John. We really appreciate you doing this, but can I call you right back? We're on our way from Lansing and getting off for some coffee." Parker had no such thoughts until that very moment. He would need to check in with Mansfield at NSA.

"That's fine. I will be awake for another couple of hours," Stanley responded.

"Thanks, John. Be right back." Parker ended the call and pointed to the exit ramp. "Tim Horton's."

John Brooks didn't mind. The idea of a Tim Horton's coffee sounded good.

"What's up?" Brooks asked as he waited at the light before turning west on M-32.

"Stanley's made contact with Sir Edward. He's supposed to meet him at Heathrow and travel to Turkmenistan with another group in Sir Edward's private jet." Parker was looking at the passing traffic in front of him.

"That's Mansfield's call," Brooks said as the light turned green and he turned left and drove under the I-75 overpass.

"I know. You or me?" Parker asked.

"You, man. You're back in service," Brooks said sarcastically with a smile as he turned left into Tim Horton's parking lot.

"Sure. Right," Parker said as Brooks hopped out of the truck and slammed the door. "Hey! Shit!" Parker yelled as he tried to get John's attention. He had to hop out and yell again before Brooks went in the side door of the restaurant. "Hey, I need your phone. Mine is mine and not secure."

Brooks threw his phone at Parker. "It's the first speed dial number." He walked inside the restaurant.

"What the hell am I doing?" Parker said to himself as he pushed the number. He waited. "I'm a damn poet. I'm supposed to be a writer not a … John? This is Parker not Brooks."

"Hi, Parker. Why so late?" John Mansfield was actually at home having dinner with Mrs. Mansfield—a rare occasion.

"It's John Stanley. He says he's supposed to meet Sir Edward in London and then proceed into Turkmenistan on Sir Edward's private jet with some others." Parker was watching Brooks point at the donuts he wanted.

"Parker, you have to make sure John Stanley does not go to Turkmenistan." Mansfield was matter-of-fact.

"Okay. I suspect I shouldn't ask why?"

"Just make sure he stays in London," Mansfield was unwavering.

"That's the message I'll deliver. Billionaires are used to making their own plans."

"Parker, this will all be over soon. Hang in there. Oh, if you haven't heard, Coruthers is dead."

Silence from Parker as he listened to Mansfield. Brooks re-entered the truck with two coffees and a bag of donuts. He saw Parker's blank stare.

"That's interesting, John. I'll let Brooks know." Parker finally responded as he slowly turned toward Brooks and grabbed his black coffee. The call ended.

"What's up now? Serious, I take it." Brooks was already rummaging through the bag for a Bavarian cream.

"Coruthers is dead. House explosion from natural gas," Parker said as he took the lid off the coffee.

"Sounds like our Russian friend." Brooks bit into the donut and started the engine. "Everybody's dead, Parker. Best part, we didn't do it."

"Pat Coruthers, president and CEO of GRR and front man for RFA, hoisted by his own petard." Parker grabbed a nutty donut.

"Yeah, and something is still rotten in Denmark," Brooks said as he looked in the rearview mirror to back up. He had the donut in the hand on the steering wheel and his coffee in the other.

"Speaking of the primrose path, I better get back to John Stanley." Parker set his coffee and donut down on the console and dialed the phone. "John, when you get to Heathrow, tell Sir Edward you'll take your own jet into Turkmenistan because you have your own schedule to keep."

"Fine. I can do that," Stanley replied. "I assume theirs is not to reason why?"

"Theirs but to do and die. Into the valley of death, John." Parker quickly made the switch from Shakespeare to Tennyson.

Stanley chuckled and ended the call.

"Geez, Moore, who's the next poet you gonna pull outta your ass?" Brooks said laughing and almost choking on the last of his Bavarian cream.

"Once upon a midnight dreary, while I pondered weak and weary …" Parker droned on.

"He's clean, yes?" Evgeny asked his associate on the phone.

"Yes. Well, there have been things not making the news, but you don't become a billionaire like John Stanley without running over a lot of people."

"But now? Recently?" Evgeny pressed.

"He's good, sir." The associate realized his pontification was unnecessary. "But there is another matter."

"Yes?" Evgeny took a deep, impatient breath.

"That Chicago lawyer and your man that was with him, they were found dead, together."

"Sounds like you know more." Evgeny was now very interested in anything the young man from the U.S. State Department could add. Evgeny had spent a great deal of time and money propagating this relationship.

"Yes, sir," the young man stammered. "There was another man with them, a Hal Morris. The locals described Morris as the local militia commander. Can't believe we still have armed militias in the States." He was again pontificating to someone that personified the very reason for those militias–the irony of it all. "And the man, or should I say CEO, of GRR was killed in an apparent natural gas explosion."

Silence from Evgeny as he scribbled a name on paper and circled it over and over as he thought.

"Sir?" The young man waited.

"Yes. I heard you. Anything else on the dead men?" Evgeny asked quietly. His voice had become mechanical.

"The three men were assassinated. Each double tapped to the head. They were found in a truck traced to a cash payment made by GRR, but no blood in the truck. It was all well-staged."

"Thank you for the information. Your account has been increased." With that Evgeny shut his phone off and sat back in his chair.

The Moscow skyline was dark and spattered with spring snow. How life had changed since the Cold War ended and capitalism brought riches unseen since the days of the Czar. But all the money in the world couldn't change what he just heard. The fact that Dimitri Anakova was alive wasn't as disturbing as what Anakova might do next. Evgeny had hired a spy because he was an expert at disappearing, as well as an expert at making death look like an accident. The three men were not an accident, and Evgeny knew that was a direct message—a very direct message.

He gazed out his modern office window at the remnants of his past Communism and failed attempts to keep such standing in the world. He recalled his time in North Vietnam, Cuba, Grenada, Afghanistan, and all the other places he touched, believing he was doing the right thing for Mother Russia. He was much like Anakova. Sir Edward had recruited Evgeny because of that very same past, as well as his newfound billions from oil-rich lands given to him by the Soviet Union. The oil was plentiful and fracking wasn't necessary, but to keep up with the energy demands of growing Russian and Chinese economies, most of the world resorted to any means necessary—and that meant fracking. As a true capitalist, Evgeny didn't care where his money or power emanated from as long as it continued flowing–much like his oil.

He had to make a decision to chase a new threat or continue with the John Stanley meeting as if nothing happened. Evgeny wasn't sure Anakova was finished. He punched in another phone number.

"Sir Edward, there's been some disturbing news from America."

ƒ ƒ ƒ

In the basement of the NSA, the staff working for the Super PAC listened to the calls Sir Edward and Evgeny exchanged. They were stunned by the phone number listed from inside the State Department. John Mansfield had walked the stairs to the basement room to think about his next steps and what he was going to tell the Super PAC. The meeting was in an hour.

"Sir, we believe the man they're discussing is Dimitri Anakova." Evans was matter-of-fact in her report. "We've traced some aliases and

IDs he's used in the past, but we have found nothing. The closest airport to Coruthers's house is Grand Rapids. There was a man of his description around the airport earlier; however, the flight we suspect he took is heading to Venezuela."

"Uh-huh." Mansfield listened and rubbed his chin.

"We have someone waiting outside the State Department to make an arrest and someone in Venezuela who can assist. It's your call."

"Yes. Yes, I know." Mansfield was pacing the room deep in thought. "Ah, good work, Evans." The dim lights from the screens, monitors, and other electronics painted Mansfield an eerie bluish green. "Is everything else working to plan?"

"Affirmative, sir," Evans replied as she watched Mansfield carefully.

"Let's relax a little and see what happens. I'll let the group know." Mansfield left the room, shutting the door behind him. He didn't wish to terminate the State Department connection since he was also on the NSA payroll. Some things only John Mansfield knew.

He walked slowly down the hall toward the Super PAC meeting room, determined to see this to the end. He opened the door. The room was empty since he was early. He sat at the round table, wondering if all would happen as it should. The best-laid plans didn't always work, but he was confident of the field staff. The worst was always the killing. It was part of the job, but it made life difficult to then go home and act normal around friends and family. The movies made light of the human effects, but they were real and always mentally taxing.

*In a true free-market economy, the widgets that die out are replaced with widgets that create income, wealth, or add to society's self-esteem. In the United States those widgets were producing, but the profit margin was greater when produced in other lands. It took a while, but the new economy was beginning to revolve around new energy exploration and wildcatting for gas and oil by use of hydraulic fracturing; however, there was also work afoot to bring back some jobs and industries America used to be good at. John Stanley's idea was just that. His experience in oil and gas allowed him some insight into the possible difficulties those industries posed for sensitive environmental areas. New technology in building energy-efficient industry with full employment of particular regions solved job issues and protected the diverse environmental concerns one would face in a highly regulated arena like the Great Lakes. A safe combination of both would perhaps decrease interests in faraway lands as well as decrease American intervention of invented capitalism to fulfill those needs within societies that didn't want to be a part of the American Dream.*

*At least, it seemed like a good idea in Frederic, Michigan.*

# THIRTY-FIVE

**TUESDAY, APRIL 26**

SIR EDWARD WAS ON HIS LARGER JET WITH EVGENY, heading toward Turkmenistan. The Suburbans would be needed to transport the entourage for the meeting with Nazar and John Stanley, who said he would be arriving shortly after he completed an errand in London. The clearance over Russian air space was granted, and Sir Edward looked below toward a country he never would have thought he could go back to after so many missions for MI6. Evgeny looked out his own window and remembered how many times he shuffled in and out of his homeland participating on his side of the Cold War. While both gazed at the country below them, neither man could shake the events that had taken place in the small State of Michigan.

"Evgeny, be a good chap and tell me what you think we should do in Michigan. After all, it was to become our largest fracking ground." Sir Edward continued to look out his window.

"I believe we should find a new CEO for GRR and act as if nothing happened." Evgeny stretched his legs and took a deep breath of air into his large barrel chest, making him, for the moment, almost too big for the seat he was in.

"Right." Sir Edward got up and proceeded toward the counter of food and drink. "I think you're right. What of your man, Anakova?"

"He is in Venezuela. There he shall remain–dead or alive."

"Any links to RFA through these tragedies?" Sir Edward sat down with a freshly made Hendricks martini.

"Nyet. My source states all appears as normal American gunplay related to the militia movements, and Coruthers's death an accident related to a faulty natural gas line in his house."

"Fine. Fine." Sir Edward seemed to relax.

"My concern, comrade," Evgeny sat forward and looked over at Sir

Edward, "is this meeting with Nazar. Why us? Why not a cavalcade of assistants and consultants to assist with a labor matter?"

"Because, my good man, John Stanley wants to see this property in person, and I intend to make it perfect. Nazar, his paranoia aside, cannot make decisions." Sir Edward turned his gaze away from the window and looked sternly at Evgeny. "If decisions have to be made on the spot, I shall make them on the spot. John Stanley is an important addition to this cause."

"Very well, but I find it unusual to say the least." Evgeny felt uneasy –even with Anakova on another continent.

The jet flew over Russia, Kazakhstan, and between the Aral and Caspian Seas.

As Evgeny looked out his window toward the Aral Sea, he wondered if that would be the same finish for the Great Lakes, so coveted by his group and Sir Edward. The Aral, once the fourth largest lake in the world, was a decimated sewer only half its size after irrigation projects, dams, fertilizers, weapons testing, and other Soviet-led improvements. Sir Edward's plan for fracking in the Great Lakes region held similar dangers, but that was not the worry of the modern capitalist. Get what you can now was the tune of the day, and Evgeny felt the same way. He wasn't sure about that feeling from John Stanley when he met him at Heathrow. Evgeny sensed a different vision in Stanley, but couldn't account for Stanley wanting to make the trip if he thought differently.

"The Aral Sea. Do you see it?" Evgeny asked.

"I can see what's left of it. Your government thought it was doing the right thing." Sir Edward strained his neck to look out Evgeny's port window while maintaining a steady hand on the Hendricks.

"My family once held land around the far eastern shore. Now, it's dust." Evgeny got up and walked over to the counter and put some ice in a small glass. "What do you think, Sir Edward, will we make dust where we go?" Evgeny poured vodka over the ice.

"We already have, Evgeny. Where we are headed was once valuable land to farmers and other nomads. Now, it is valuable only to us."

Evgeny could feel the cold from Sir Edward today like no other day. Evgeny was the same but with a different accent; even still, Sir Edward's frigid response was cold even by Evgeny's standards.

"I guess you are correct, comrade. I drink a toast to you, and thank you for your leadership."

The two men clinked glasses and Evgeny returned to his seat. The plane was to fly over Uzbekistan before landing at the new runway near the wells of Serhetabat.

* * *

The day was like any other day for most of the three hundred million Americans. The cars were stuck in rush hour, trains stopped and started, and planes took off and landed as no one had a clue what was going to happen thousands of miles away—even though the very essence of life as they knew it would change. Stock markets would crumble. Countries would point fingers. America's energy policy would be curtailed as if strapped to a runaway elevator dropping through the floors of the Empire State Building. And all of this would be purposeful. Threats had to be met head-on. Militaries were no longer the only answer. Wars looked different. American politics and people were objects for the highest bidder.

The Director of the Super PAC, Carin Rialto, sat in her private office after the group approved the actions toward the clear and present danger to the United States of America. The President was on board. The Vice President was aware. In her role as Secretary of State under Bush 43, Rialto was a public figure seen every day and everywhere. In her new secretive role as protector of a democracy she believed in, the public never saw her. In fact, she was always amused at the tabloids and major news stations that took liberties with her pictures and quotes handed out purposely as fodder to feed the celebrity-crazy society. It actually made her job easier. She knew the U.S. would recover, and she also knew the U.S. would be one of the finger pointers.

She watched the live drone and satellite feeds on the monitors in front of her.

* * *

When the missile hit, it looked as if the wellhead right next to the private jet had exploded. In the aftermath, nothing was left and fire raged as the burning natural gas plumed high into the sky. Hades himself couldn't have put on a greater show.

The explosion startled the men of Wellhead 120. The intense heat washed over them in seconds. The only sound was the rush of fire exploding into the air from the well. It was as if the earth opened up to devour the infidels. Some men were on the ground in prayer. Others simply watched in awe. They looked around for the masked man who called for the meeting, but he was nowhere to be seen. The explosion must have consumed both him and his truck as he predicted.

The masked man looked behind him at the flames. He had driven over the runway just before the plane landed in a pretend gesture for the men watching him. He had told them he was to commit suicide by driving into the landing plane. In actuality, his trip would be long and dusty along a remnant of the original silk route and around some of the oldest known oasis settlements in the world. He took off his mask and grabbed a cell phone that was taped underneath the dashboard, well out of sight and out of reach for anyone searching the truck.

"John, I'm coming home," Todd Ramsey said quietly into the phone.

"It'll be good to see you. Brooks is on his way back to D.C. too. Parker Moore is parked at home." John Mansfield was shutting off his laptop and closing the lid as he spoke. His tie was long since removed and hung over his chair.

"This was a tough one." Ramsey smiled as he thought of the Perry Hotel and chasing Parker Moore around for nine days the previous year. "Hey, John?"

"Yeah, Todd," Mansfield said into the speaker phone as he put on his jacket.

"Why don't we just hire Moore and be done with it? He'd be easier to get rid of that way." Ramsey laughed as he bounced along the old highway.

"That's a good idea, Todd. We may just have to do that."

# THIRTY-SIX

IT WAS AFTER MIDNIGHT. COLD TEMPS HAD RETURNED and the wind had the bay whipped into a frenzy. Every seasonal change equaled wind. Parker was reading Emerson's *Nature* while Sam lay next to him reading the paper. It was well after her bedtime, but she had things to say.

"The change is in the air," Sam said while reading the editorial in the *Petoskey News & Review*.

"Hmm." Parker breathed out.

"Change. Really. People are willing to make sacrifices to keep Michigan clean and protect the waters," Sam continued still gazing at the paper.

"How so?" Parker looked up from his book and over at Sam. His glasses parked down on his nose.

The wind howled through the window. Kali and Keeper ran out of the bedroom with the sudden blast of cold air hitting them square as they did their best sphinx impressions on the bed.

"This editorial suggests that, at least in Emmet County, fracking should be halted and banned because of the proximity to so much of our water. The bay, the Straits, all the rivers and streams, and even the Neo-Cons are questioning the safety after the press release from the governor's office alarming us to the poison chemicals in the Manistee River."

"Really? Hmm." Parker was back at the book.

"By the way," Sam put down the paper, "some anonymous caller notified the Department of Environmental Quality about the sheen in the river from Dorian Gray's place all the way south of County Road 612. The Department also found samples of water from the river on their doorstep one morning at their office in Gaylord." Sam was now sitting up in bed. "There's another note in the paper today about a John Stanley press release discussing the new green factories he's building in the state beginning with Frederic."

"Wow. That's great. Bad thing about that water. Good thing about your newfound friends in Frederic." Parker never took his eyes off the pages. When lost in *Nature*, he was lost.

"Parker," Sam started again as she grabbed Parker's right arm and shook it. "I also got a call from the governor's office today."

"About?" He looked over.

"Fracking. They want me, or should I say, he wants me to head a new taskforce on limiting fracking in Michigan and devising a plan for its eventual elimination." Sam was smiling through furled eyebrows and a wrinkled forehead.

"That's great, honey." Parker put down his book and smiled. "You deserve that call after your hard work. You have been through the ringer for that cause."

Sam gazed at Parker. She looked at him and realized the change. Parker's recovery from the abuse and a world of deception was complete. His demeanor was relaxed and confident, but most of all she noticed an ease of manner. Humor and patience took the place of the fear and frantic he'd experienced not so long ago. It was as if he was fully resurrected and recreated.

"You, ah, wouldn't have anything to do with any of this?" Sam leaned over and kissed Parker on the cheek and whispered in his ear.

"Me? Nah. I'm just a poet and a writer." Parker put his face back in the book, pretending to ignore Sam's tenderness, but it was difficult. His favorite thing in the world, something that had taken him so long to get in life, was a simple kiss on the cheek. He always equated that with true and authentic affection.

"The paper also said there were samples of the river water delivered to every major newspaper in the state with a record of where it came from and a map of the testing site north of Cameron Bridge Road in the Deward Preserve between Gaylord and Frederic," Sam continued to whisper.

"I'll be damned. That's interesting. What a coincidence with the governor, eh?" Parker continued to look at his page. He wasn't reading.

"Oh," Sam sat up and grabbed Parker's book. "And, where's my car?"

"It's in the garage."

"No. There's a brand-new Ford Escape in there." Sam looked as angry as she could without breaking out in laughter.

"New car? Oh, the Escape? Yeah, Steve Brown thought someone who was a regular visitor to the governor's office should have a new Ford. You know, some real Detroit metal. Oh, and it's a hybrid. Your Honda wouldn't do," Parker said. "You know," he sat up straight and acted as if he had an epiphany, "it must have been Steve Brown who did all that stuff with the water and called the governor. Why would he give, er, sell us the car?"

"Oh, yeah. I'll have to thank him tomorrow," Sam said as she pushed Parker down on his pillow. She snuggled onto Parker's chest and put her right hand over him, rubbing his left shoulder while he picked the book back up off the nightstand. Emerson was Parker's true inspiration, and she understood the connection it held this night with the topic at hand.

The wind howled as the season continued to change–right along with Parker.

# ABOUT THE AUTHOR

STEWERT JAMES really does spend many a day visiting Roast & Toast and Chandlers. He continues his quiet serenity overlooking Little Traverse Bay and Lake Michigan; and makes regular pilgrimages to the Dune's Saloon, Lake Superior, Frederic, and fly-fishing the Manistee River.